She couldn't do it.

Couldn't risk her heart again, she wasn't sure she could find her way back one more time. So she'd help Rett and baby Ryann get settled, to bond, and then she'd make a graceful exit.

So she pasted on a smile and prepared to play nice as she rang the doorbell to Rett's home.

Of course he answered the door in a pair of gray sweatpants and nothing else, a screaming Ryann held against his bare chest.

"Thank God," he said, and thrust the baby into her arms.

"Oh, goodness. It's okay, baby." Skye immediately focused on Ryann, soothing her quietly and rubbing her back. The twenty-three-month-old felt too light in Skye's arms.

When Ryann calmed enough to recognize a new voice and body, she leaned back to see who held her. She blinked her tear-wet blue eyes.

"Mama?" she asked hopefully.

Heart sad, Skye shook her head, unable to say the words that Cassie was gone.

Ryann's little face crumpled, she lay her head on Skye's shoulder and sobbed and sobbed.

Skye met Rett's gaze, found patience and understanding.

She stepped inside. "I need to talk to you."

Dear Reader,

I believe that love and family conquers all. And I do love to throw my characters into instant family situations. What more emotional circumstances are there? When a child's welfare is involved, the stakes are immediately high. The risks are high, but so are the payoffs.

The Sullivans are six brothers that have a strong family bond who have each had to deal with becoming a father before he was ready. Finding the love of his life has completed Rett's new family. Rett is the final brother and his journey highlights these concepts in a poignant, uplifting conclusion to the series. I hope you have enjoyed reading about the Sullivans as much as I've enjoyed bringing you their stories.

Teresa

TERESA CARPENTER
The Playboy's Gift

TORONTO NEW YORK LONDON
AMSTERDAM PARIS SYDNEY HAMBURG
STOCKHOLM ATHENS TOKYO MILAN MADRID
PRAGUE WARSAW BUDAPEST AUCKLAND

Recycling programs
for this product may
not exist in your area.

ISBN-13: 978-0-373-17764-6

THE PLAYBOY'S GIFT

First North American Publication 2011

Copyright © 2011 by Teresa Carpenter

Teresa Carpenter believes in the power of unconditional love, and that there's no better place to find it than between the pages of a romance novel. Reading is a passion for Teresa—a passion that led to a calling. She began writing more than twenty years ago, and marks the sale of her first book as one of her happiest memories. Teresa gives back to her craft by volunteering her time to Romance Writers of America on a local and national level.

A fifth-generation Californian, she lives in San Diego, within miles of her extensive family, and knows with their help she can accomplish anything. She takes particular joy and pride in her nieces and nephews, who are all bright, fit, shining stars of the future. If she's not at a family event, you'll usually find her at home—reading, writing or playing with her adopted Chihuahua, Jefe.

"Teresa Carpenter's *Her Baby, His Proposal* makes an oft-used premise work brilliantly through skilled plotting, deft characterisation and just the right amount of humor."
—*RT Book Reviews*

To my family, each and every one.
I would not be me without all of you.
Thank you for your love and support.

In memory of Ryan West,
may he rest in peace.

And for Ryann Sanaa West, his namesake
and our latest pride and joy.

CHAPTER ONE

"THANK YOU for coming, Ms. Miller." The attorney motioned for Skye to take a seat in one of the beige armchairs facing his desk. "I know this is a difficult time."

Yes, a very difficult time. Ten months after her brother Aidan's death, they'd buried her sister-in-law, Cassie. Rare as it was in this day and age, Skye believed her brother's widow died of a broken heart. Cassie fell into a depression after Aidan's death and never quite pulled herself out of it.

Now Skye numbly sat down across from the lawyer prepared to discuss custody of her orphaned niece, the beautiful toddler Skye hadn't allowed herself to love.

"I don't really understand why I'm here," she stated as she settled into the leather chair. "I thought Cassie's parents would take Ryann."

"I'll explain everything in a few minutes," Phil Bourne assured her. "We're waiting for another party. Ah, here he is."

"Skye." Warm, strong hands cupped her shoulders and squeezed.

Rett Sullivan. Aidan's best friend. And her first love.

The one person who would understand how much she hurt. The one person she'd taught herself to forget.

Suddenly it was too much and the tears she'd held at bay for so long rose up threatening to overcome her. She bowed her head, fighting for composure.

"I'll give you a few minutes." The attorney stepped out of the room.

"I know how alone you must feel." Rett hunkered down beside her. A tall, dark-haired man, his broad shoulders filled her vision while his familiar blue eyes snagged her light brown gaze. "I hope you know you can always call me. The Sullivans consider you family."

Of course. The Sullivans.

"Than—" Her throat closed up, and she finished with a nod.

"Aw, babe." He tucked the fall of her hair behind her ear. "I miss him, too."

She squeezed her eyes closed her, tried to breathe. But it was too much; she'd held the tears back too long. With a stifled sob, she rose intending to push past him for a moment of privacy and stepped into his arms instead.

Immediately he enveloped her in an embrace of strength and warmth. He crushed her to him, threading his fingers in her short black hair to hold her close. She clung to him even as her composure splintered and broke.

And then she felt the wetness against her temple. Oh, God. Tears flowed as evidence of his sorrow broke through her numbness. In the heat and comfort of his arms she let the grief consume her.

Skye didn't know how long they cried together, but for that short time she didn't feel so alone. He smelled so good, of soap, man and a hint of spice; so familiar and a little like coming home.

"I miss him so much," she said on a shuddering breath. "And now Cassie's gone, too."

"I know."

"I can't believe I've lost them both."

"They're not gone as long as we have our memories."

Okay that would sound hokey from anyone but Rett, who came from a large, close-knit family that had known its fair share of loss. It was meant to comfort, for that reason it helped. But not much.

Nothing really helped, except not feeling.

"It's not the same."

"No." He agreed and left it at that. Because truly what more could he say?

She took a half step back and looked up into his blue eyes, the power of them made stronger by the evidence of his grief. Tall and broad shouldered, he tempted her to lean on him. She'd known him for more than twenty-five years, loved him for a part of that time, but he hadn't been in her life for a long time.

There was too much history, too much pain between them for them ever to be easy with each other. She'd reconciled herself to that fact a long time ago.

But in these minutes of shared grief she welcomed

his presence, took comfort in his nearness. That is why she pushed away and squared her shoulders.

"I'm fine now. Thank you." She snagged a couple of tissues from the box on the attorney's desk.

He accepted a tissue but watched her carefully. "Nobody expects you to be strong every moment."

"And crying solves nothing. Excuse me, I'm going to freshen up." She looked around for her purse. "Tell the attorney I'll be back in a few minutes."

In the small bathroom she rinsed her hands and face with cold water. It helped to restore her composure. New makeup and a few minutes alone helped more. An answer to the question looping through her head would be even more helpful.

Why was Rett here for a conversation about Ryann?

With her mask back in place, she tucked her purse under her arm and returned to Mr. Bourne's office to find her answers.

"Rett Sullivan, the designer." She heard the attorney talking to Rett as she approached. "From Sullivans' Jewels right?"

"Yes." Rett acknowledged the connection. "My brother Rick handles the business side. Aidan Miller was manager of the downtown store."

"I bought my wife's engagement ring at Sullivans'. You're good, not the same cookie-cutter stuff as everyone else."

"We try."

"I'm sorry for keeping you waiting." The men rose

when Skye entered the room. She took her seat and began by repeating her earlier comment.

"Mr. Bourne, please tell us why we're here. As I mentioned, I thought Cassie's parents were taking Ryann."

"Actually no. Mr. Gleason suffered a stroke a couple of years ago plus they're older. They don't feel they can handle a toddler. They'll be happy with regular visits." Phil leaned back in his chair and met their gazes across the desk. "Cassie has left custody of Ryann to the two of you."

Skye blinked at him then bowed her head to hide her expression. The news rocked her to her soul. How could Cassie do this to her? The betrayal was like tearing a bandage off a fresh wound.

With Rett sitting next to her, the past rushed toward her releasing all the painful emotions long suppressed, the disappointment, the lost hope, the betrayal. The loss.

So much loss over the years.

There must be some mistake. She couldn't do this.

"Ms. Miller? Ms. Miller, are you okay?" The attorney called for her attention. "Can I get you some coffee or perhaps a water?"

"What?" Startled, she blinked him into focus. "Oh. I'm sorry." She declined the offer of refreshments with a shake of her head. She knew she must be white; she'd felt the blood leave her cheeks. Maybe that's why she couldn't think—her brain was deprived of oxygen. Maybe it had nothing to do with the fact her niece had just been placed in her care.

"Please continue. As you can tell, I'm surprised. Mr.

Sullivan and I are not a couple. And neither of us has spent much time with Ryann."

"As an only child, Cassie's options were limited, but she was confident in her decision."

"How could she be? I'm not equipped to raise her, and I wouldn't trust Rett with a puppy—"

"Hey," Rett protested.

"Sorry." She spared him a glance. "But we both know you're a player and haven't had the care of a child for more than an hour or two your whole life."

Rett shrugged. He couldn't deny her claim. But while she didn't know why he was here, he did.

This wasn't part of the plan. Aidan wasn't supposed to die. Rett wasn't supposed to raise Ryann. Skye wasn't supposed to get hurt. It all caused Rett's head to spin.

"Cassie was comfortable with her choice because she felt you would both have been Aidan's choice. If you refuse to take this on, Ryann will end up in foster care."

"The Gleasons—"

"—may agree to take her, but it's my belief Child Services will agree with their original assessment that they're too elderly."

"Child Services will be evaluating us?"

"It's standard, yes."

"Right." Skye popped to her feet and began to pace. "I loved my brother, but I have a one bedroom apartment. How is this going to work?"

Bourne shuffled papers. "Ryann has a healthy trust account that can be used for her care."

"I have plenty of money," Rett interjected. "There's no need to touch Ryann's account."

Skye turned to him. "You're seriously considering doing this? You know your entire life is going to change?"

"What choice do we have?" Rett caught himself tapping his thigh in a mindless beat, a sure sign of his restlessness. He clinched his hand into a fist and rested it on the arm of the chair. All these formalities chafed his nerves. "The Gleasons are good people, but I agree a toddler is too much for them to handle full-time. We can't let her go into foster care."

"Rick and his wife can take her." Skye offered up Rett's twin brother who was married with a son about to turn one. "Or one of your other brothers."

"No. It has to be me. What's wrong, Skye? Is this about what happened fifteen years ago?" Of course it was. If the past was in his thoughts, it had to be in hers.

Her scathing glare nearly burned his retinas.

"It's not irrelevant. Fate made it pretty clear we were not a good parent combo."

"You were never a fatalist before."

A scoffing laugh escaped her. And her teeth snapped as if she'd bit back a caustic comment. He sympathized; she had had a tough year. Heck when it came to loss of loved ones, she'd had a tough life starting with her mother when she was only six.

"That was a long time ago. Obviously fate has a new message for us courtesy of Cassie. I can't let Ryann go into foster care, Skye."

Then you can take her, Rett knew the words hovered on the tip of her tongue. He gave her points for swallowing them.

"Why does it have to be you?"

"What?"

"Rick was Aidan's friend, too. We both know he would take Ryann. You said it had to be you. Why?"

Rett silently cursed. He should have known she was too smart to fool. So truth or lie? He wasn't against prevaricating to save her from being hurt, but he didn't relish starting a partnership with her based on a lie.

Damn, why hadn't Aidan told her? Because there was no way Rett could tell her now without hurting her. And she'd already suffered so much.

It felt like a bitter betrayal from a man he still mourned. He was so angry. His muscles twitched with the desire to see his buddy across the ring, to go a few rounds pounding on each other until someone came out smarter than they went in.

Too late for that now. Now he needed to think about Ryann.

"Because she's my daughter."

CHAPTER TWO

Skye went completely still, she couldn't have heard what she thought she did. "Aidan was Ryann's father."

"No."

"Of course he was." Denial was strong and immediate as a myriad of emotions roiled inside her. Confusion, hurt, betrayal, love, regret, anger.

"Skye." Rett stood and moved toward her, trying to take her hands. She jerked back, swaying from him.

He sighed.

"You know Aidan and Cassie had trouble conceiving." He reminded her.

"Yes." Her heart sped as realization dawned. "They used a donor." She took a deep breath, letting it out slowly. If she was going to make it through this, she needed to stay calm. "You."

"Yes."

Bourne stood up behind his desk. "I'll give you two a few minutes."

"That's not necessary," she advised him. "I'm leaving." Swinging around she grabbed her purse, got up and made for the door.

"Skye, wait." Rett followed on her heels. In the outer office he grabbed her hand. "Don't go."

She shook him off, and hit the outside door. "Leave me alone."

"Skye, please don't go." He cut her off in the building courtyard. "I'm sorry you had to find out like this. I'm sorry our past makes this difficult. But there is a bigger issue here."

"Right. Your daughter."

"Yes. And God, do you have any idea how strange it is for me to say that? Do you think this is easy for me? This was never supposed to happen."

"Oh, yeah, poor Rett. I don't think Aidan or Cassie are too happy, either."

"You're right. But I'm trying to do the right thing here. Ryann is the innocent one in all this. Don't make this about us."

Memories of her miscarriage rose up to haunt her, the grief mixed with relief. The loss of the child always connected in her mind with the loss of the man who'd been both friend and lover.

And now another child linked them together.

His child with another woman.

That shouldn't have the power to hurt her, but it did.

"Oh, God." She slowly sank onto a stone bench surrounding a fountain. The stone was as cold as she felt. "You take her then. You don't need me."

"I do need you. You're right when you say I've never watched a kid more than an hour or two. And that's been rare. But more important Ryann needs you. You're her family."

"But I'm not, am I?" And why did that hurt so much when she'd never allowed herself to connect too closely with Ryann? Sure, Skye saw the kid when she visited her brother, and she'd babysat a few times, but Skye always kept her emotions in check.

"Family is not just about blood."

She rubbed a thumb over her forehead where a headache beat just under the surface. He was asking too much. Every time she held Ryann she'd be reminded of the child she lost.

"Your sisters-in-law can help you."

"It's not that simple," he assured her. "They have families of their own, and full-time jobs. I'm sure they'll help where they can, but Ryann is comfortable with you." He sat beside her. "Can you really walk away from Aidan's daughter? I provided some DNA, he idolized her."

He had her there. Aidan had been her big brother, her hero. She'd never forgive herself if she let him down now.

"Please come back inside. Let's finish hearing what the attorney has to say."

She inclined her head. Allowed him to lead her back to the office and Bourne.

Standing at the window, arms crossed in front of her, as if holding herself together, she asked, "So how do we do this?"

The attorney basically repeated what he'd already

outlined and added a reminder that Child Services would be contacting them.

"The caseworker is assigned to Ryann. They can make unscheduled visits to your home, your child care, even your work. Their job is to make sure Ryann is in a safe, supportive environment. My best advice is to be yourselves."

"Right." Rett scowled but nodded. "It sounds like I have the bigger place, so I'll take her first."

"If I can offer some more advice." Bourne leaned forward. "Ryann is already traumatized. I have kids and I can tell you change can be upsetting. I'd suggest setting her up in one residence until she gets over…ah, accustomed to the two of you."

"So it's final then?" Rett demanded. "Ryann is ours now?"

"Yes. She's with the Gleasons. All you have to do is pick her up."

Skye's cell vibrated for the third time in as many minutes. She didn't generally answer her phone while she was working but she'd left it on because she had Ryann to think of now.

And she had no doubt who was trying to get hold of her. Rett had already called her to find out if Ryann took a bottle and what she ate.

Skye had gone straight from the appointment at the attorney's to the rehearsal dinner she was shooting tonight so she hadn't been with Rett when he picked up Ryann.

Now he had her on speed dial.

"Rett." Skye stepped to the back of the room to take the call. "I'm trying to work here."

"I wouldn't call if I didn't need help." Rett sounded desperate. "She hasn't stopped crying since I picked her up." Ryann's cries came through the line. "And she keeps asking for her mother."

"She's traumatized. You just have to have patience."

"I bypassed patient an hour ago. I'm strung tighter than a high wire."

She sighed. She was sure he was. Her own nerves were at a breaking point. For that reason and because she should be there helping him she relented.

"What do you need?"

"I'm changing her diaper. I need you to walk me through it."

"Seriously?" What was there to know; you took off the dirty one and replaced it with a clean one. Obviously more than his nerves were frazzled. She drew on some patience of her own. "Is she wearing a diaper or pull-ups?"

"What? I don't know. What's the difference?"

"Cassie was starting to potty train her. Diapers have flaps. Pull-ups are disposable panties."

"She's wearing diapers."

"Okay." Skye walked him through the diaper change and then said, "She's probably as exhausted as you are. Try giving her a juice cup in a darkened room, maybe put some music on low."

"Do you think that will put her to sleep?" Despair sounded clear in his voice.

"Let's hope so." She tried to put optimism in her response. "If not, give me a call and I'll come by when I'm done here."

"You can count on it." The cries grew louder and she guessed he'd picked Ryann up. "Thanks for your help."

The line went dead and her cell informed her the call was ended.

Skye went back to work silently praying for all their sakes that Ryann got some sleep.

Skye stomped up the path to Rett's front door.

Damn. Damn. Damn.

The thought of letting Rett back into her life upset Skye as much as the thought of taking on Ryann. She'd fought hard over the past ten years to find a place of peace within herself impervious to hurt.

You could only lose so much before you shut down emotionally and she hit that after her split from her ex. Losing Aidan and then Cassie were timely reminders that caring just opened you to more pain.

She'd had a rehearsal dinner to shoot Friday night and a wedding on Saturday so she'd told Rett she'd be over on Sunday. She'd brooded while working, tried to envision what life would be like with Ryann, and the picture nearly sent her into panic mode.

She couldn't do it. Couldn't risk her heart again, she wasn't sure she could find her way back one more time.

So she'd help Rett and Ryann get settled, to bond, and then she'd make a graceful exit.

Of course that meant putting up with Rett, but Skye would handle it. After all, the past was over and done, right? She didn't have to be his friend; she just had to be cordial.

That was her plan: leave the past out of it, maintain an emotional distance and push Rett and Ryann together as much as possible.

So she pasted on a smile and prepared to play nice as she rang the doorbell to Rett's home. His house was a sprawling one-story ranch in Point Loma, a lovely, well-established, well-to-do neighborhood at the very tip of San Diego.

Of course he answered the door in a pair of gray sweatpants and nothing else, a screaming Ryann held against his bare chest.

"Thank God," he said and thrust the baby into her arms.

"Oh, goodness. It's okay, baby." Skye immediately focused on Ryann, soothing her quietly and rubbing her back. The twenty-three-month-old felt too light in Skye's arms.

When Ryann calmed enough to recognize a new voice and body, she leaned back to see who held her. She blinked tear wet blue eyes.

"Mama?" she asked hopefully.

Heart-sad Skye shook her head unable to say the words that Cassie was gone.

Ryann's little face crumpled, she laid her head on Skye's shoulder and sobbed and sobbed.

Skye met Rett's gaze, found patience and understanding.

"I know," he acknowledged, reaching out to slide a hand down Ryann's baby-fine brown hair. "It breaks your heart."

It truly did. Not even Skye was immune to the baby's obvious pain. Holding the little girl, rocking her gently, Skye sought something—anything—to distract herself. Her gaze snagged on Rett's bare feet. The lack of shoes didn't surprise her. If he were at home, he'd be without shoes. As for the rest, she tried not to stare at the tanned beauty of his broad shoulders, strong abs and ripped biceps.

Not exactly the distraction she would have chosen, but his fine, hard body made it difficult to look away.

He'd obviously run his hands through his mink-brown hair because it was swept back and tousled. Not at all his normal sleek self. Rett believed appearance mattered.

"So, Skye." He stared at her and then looked at the street behind her and frowned.

She followed his steel-blue gaze but saw nothing of interest. Turning back, she found the frown was now leveled at her. She ran her hand over Ryann's back, and met him stare for stare.

"So, Rett." She angled her head. "Were you expecting someone else?"

"Pizza delivery. We're both starved but she's been so

upset I barely managed the time to dial for the pizza."
He pulled away from the support of the doorjamb and
waved her over the threshold.

She stepped inside. "I need to talk to you."

"Before you start railing, let me assure you it's not
my fault."

"Of course it's your fault." She followed him into a
room done in shades of blue and gray, the colors of the
sea in sunshine and storm. The decor showcased the
magnificent ocean view out the huge picture window.
His taste ran to modern and comfort, sharp lines but
lush fabrics and deep cushions. Hard surfaces gleamed
or shined.

He dropped onto a dark gray couch and flung an arm
over his brow.

"You had to—" she waved a hand toward him "—do
your thing."

He lifted his arm to pin her with weary blue eyes.
"It's not my fault you didn't know. I figured Aidan
would have told you."

She settled in a wide, armless chair in soft silver and
settled Ryann in her lap. The child burrowed close and
Skye held her lightly. "That you'd be having a child with
my sister-in-law?" she asked, proud of the steadiness
in her voice. "No, my brother failed to share that little
detail."

"I'm sorry. But that's on him."

He was right and the betrayal stung anew. "You could
have told me."

"Our conversations surrounding babies don't tend to go too well."

Another truth. Another sharp sting.

There was a husky rasp to Rett's voice, a disturbingly sexy rasp that distracted her from the conversation. Shoring up her control, she squared her shoulders and refocused her attention.

"What's wrong with you?" Annoyance mixed with concern, she didn't want to care about him. Didn't want to be here at all.

"I'm fine." He dismissed his illness. "It's just a cold trying to take hold."

"Idiot. If you have a cold, you're not fine." She rose, and reluctantly approached his half naked body. She tested his temperature with a hand on his forehead. "You are a little warm."

Well, that explained why he was half naked in the middle of the day.

He opened his eyes to flash her a glance. "Thanks for the news flash."

"Smart-ass. Are you taking anything for it?"

He waved vaguely indicating the back of the house. "I'm probably due for another dose." He closed his eyes again. "Sorry. I'm not at my best. My head feels like a sledgehammer is running full tilt."

Suddenly Ryann pushed away from Skye. "Mama," she wailed, fresh tears streaming down her face.

Rett flinched.

Skye stood to pace, gently rocking the little girl in her arms, humming softly. When Ryann refused to be soothed, Skye flashed a glance at Rett. He now sat forward on the sofa, hands clasped in front of him, gaze fixed on her and Ryann.

"Well, you're going to have to suck it up," she told him. "Grab a T-shirt and shoes. We'll take her for a ride. That should put her to sleep for a while."

"Go ahead. I've had her for two days. It's your turn now."

"Oh, no. You were the one so eager to do this. I'm here to help, not to take over."

"Be a sport. I'm sick."

"You just said you were fine."

"Come on, I need some rest."

"And I needed to work this afternoon, but I'm here. Move your butt."

"Well, since you asked so nicely." He surged to his feet and headed for the back of the house. The heaviness of his movements told her more than anything else how off he was feeling. Lithe and strong, he usually moved with more confidence and grace.

For all his arguments he seemed relieved by the action. That fit. The Rett she'd known hadn't done helpless very well. He was hardwired to go for the fix. In this instance there was no easy solution. Only time would cure Ryann's heartache. What she needed most was patience, understanding and love.

Skye hoped he did better by Ryann than he had by her.

Skye followed him down the hall looking for Ryann's room to change her and grab her diaper bag. She went past a home office, an in-house gym, a workshop/studio and a media room. All the rooms were tastefully appointed with solid furniture and vivid textures. But there was no sign of Ryann in any of them. Skye returned to the living room and found the diaper bag near the chair where she'd been sitting.

She had the baby changed and ready when Rett returned dressed in a red polo shirt and blue jeans. She handed him the diaper bag and they walked to the driveway where a slick sports car sat beside a massive Cadillac EXT. Rett strapped Ryann in her seat and Skye climbed into the front of the four-door SUV/truck, noting the new car smell. A few minutes later they were on the road.

Ryann continued to whine while Rett made his way to Freeway 8, but once the vehicle hit the open highway, she quickly dozed off.

Eyes straight ahead, hands clasped in her lap, Skye asked. "What makes you think I was going to yell?"

She felt the weight of his gaze before he turned it back to the road.

"Because according to Aidan, you believe I'm responsible for everything bad to happen in the last fifty years, from the Vietnam War, to 9/11, to the killer bees migrating up from Mexico."

"That's ridiculous. You haven't even been alive for fifty years."

Why would Aidan say such a thing? She'd only blamed Rett for one thing: breaking her heart. Perhaps this had been Aidan's way of protecting her from further heartache. Perhaps whenever Rett asked after her, Aidan had discouraged him by professing her dislike.

"That's what I said." Rett coughed, the sound drawing her gaze. He rolled his head, stretching his neck one way and then the other, fighting off fatigue.

She frowned, disturbed by the signs of his lethargy. He radiated a heat that had nothing to do with a low-grade fever and everything to do with her body recognizing his. Chemistry had never been their problem.

Exactly how often had he asked after her?

Deciding that was a question best left alone, she asked instead, "Did you take some medicine?"

"I'm fine," he declared before snagging her gaze with piercing blue eyes. "I know you're having trouble with this whole thing, but I need you to get over it already."

CHAPTER THREE

THE CALLOUSNESS OF his words nearly knocked Skye back in her seat. Dear Lord, going ten rounds with a champion prizefighter couldn't hurt more.

Obviously the loss of their child hadn't haunted him through the years as it had her.

She held on to her composure by a thread. It seemed every time she found her feet, she got pounded by another mental blow. She felt exposed, emotionally bruised, raw.

Still, she lifted her chin, unwilling to let him see her pain.

"Says the man who begged for my help. Remind me again why I agreed."

"Because this is Aidan's fault and he's not here so you're stuck cleaning up his messes."

"You're the one with the duty complex."

"And you could have just walked away and let Ryann go into foster care?"

She turned to look out the window, seeing nothing. How did she answer that without sounding like a cold-hearted bitch? With the truth, much as it hurt to admit.

"No. I couldn't have walked away."

"Then can you drop the attitude so we can begin working together here? I have work, too. And other pursuits—unlike you—that have all had to take a backseat these last few days."

"Poor Rett, feeling the chafe of fatherhood."

"At least I'm not marrying a dweeb to solve my problems."

She flinched at the jab at their past. Dweeb was Aidan's word for her ex. But she wasn't going there with Rett.

"My life is none of your business." She hugged herself feeling the need to hold on to something. She had no defense against his claim. Work was her life; it was safer viewed through the lenses of her camera.

"No. But Ryann's is."

"She's an obligation to you." She bit out, forcing herself to relax her defensive pose. "Don't pretend otherwise."

"Skye." He reached for her hand.

She pulled her fingers away. "Don't even think about it."

His hands clenched on the wheel.

"Look, I know you're feeling very alone. But this will be easier if we work together. We can establish a schedule and both get our lives back."

"You could hire a nanny and leave me out of it."

"Not going to happen." It wasn't harshly stated, but there was no give in it, either. "The nanny is not a bad idea, but Ryann needs you."

"You can't count on me. I could move away," she said through gritted teeth, "or marry another dweeb."

He shook his head. "I'm willing to chance it." He surprised her by snagging her left hand from her lap. His fingers wrapped around hers and he held her hand in the heat of his, squeezing lightly. "She's my daughter, Skye."

"You keep saying that as if it means something to you." The bitterness tasted sour, but she couldn't help how she felt. She tugged at her hand but he held her secure.

"You know it does. Family is important to me."

"Raising a child requires more than a sense of duty." She waved her free hand indicating the direction they'd come from. "Your place is a bachelor pad on steroids. You don't even have a guest room."

"What?" He slanted a cool glance her way. "Were you snooping while I was changing?"

She lifted her chin and met him glare for glare. "I was looking for somewhere to change Ryann, so, yeah, I checked out the rooms down the hall."

One thick, dark eyebrow lifted. "Right."

"I glanced in a few open doors. I didn't paw through your drawers." She yanked at her hand again demanding release.

"And yet you feel qualified to criticize?"

"Yes, actually. There was no crib, no changing table, no dresser. I found what I needed in her diaper bag, but what's going to happen when those supplies run out?"

"I have a suitcase and some supplies in my room. Not that I owe you any explanations."

Frustrated, she looked away, drew in a deep breath, counted to five as she exhaled. Calmer, she met his gaze again.

"Let. Me. Go."

Eyes amused, he shook his head and stroked his thumb over the sensitive flesh of her palm.

The small caress of rough skin over soft sent a sensual shiver down her spine. Damn him.

"Does being near me bother you?" he asked in a throaty whisper.

"Being in the same state with you bothers me. Try to stay on topic."

"Why didn't you answer my calls?" He threaded his fingers through hers, creating an intimacy she struggled to ignore.

"What?" But she knew. He'd called three times since Aidan's funeral. She glanced down at her lap. "I didn't think we had anything to talk about."

"We've been friends since we were ten years old."

"I was seven, and that was a long time ago. We're not the same people anymore."

"You were six. But you always did like to round your age up."

"Not anymore, which only proves my point that we've changed." Turning back to him, she demanded. "I need you to let me go."

He sighed. "I can't. The truth is I need you. I'm going to raise my daughter. But I don't know what I'm doing and she's the one suffering for it. I don't want some nanny coming in and taking over. And I don't want my family pitying me."

His stark honesty touched something buried deep inside her that demanded an honest response.

"I'm afraid of being hurt again," she whispered past the constriction in her throat.

He went still and then inclined his head. "Skye, you have to know I never meant to hurt you—"

"Not you." She shot him a get real glance. "Ryann. I can't love her. I can't lose another child."

He spread her fingers, placed her hand over his heart and released her. "I'm not the villain here, Skye."

"Damn you." She curled her fingers into a fist, hit him once and then dropped her arm. Of course she'd love Ryann—she was sweet, and happy and beautiful. And he didn't care how it would tear her apart. "I can't do this."

Suddenly they'd pulled onto the side of the road and he'd swept her into his arms. He held her though she struggled weakly. Just weary, she sagged against him. In a minute she'd continue fighting. In a minute, when he didn't expect it, she'd break away from the hard comfort of his arms, the soft touch of his hand stroking her hair.

"Don't be nice to me, Rett. I'm pretty sure you had something to do with that whole killer bee thing."

His hold tightened around her and she felt him smile against her temple.

"I'm just a simple jeweler. I don't know about such things."

Because it felt too good leaning against him, she pushed away.

"Simple has never been a word I'd use to describe you." And he was being modest. Sullivans' Jewels owed as much of its success to Rett's spectacular designs and workmanship as it did to his twin brother's brilliant business sense. Together they'd boosted the family owned store to international acclaim.

A coughing attack suddenly racked his body. He returned to his seat where he snagged a tissue from the console and blew his nose. Clearing his throat he looked over his shoulder to check on Ryann. When he faced forward again, she saw the toll the cold had taken on his energy.

After checking his mirrors, he put the truck in gear and pulled back onto the highway.

Skye shifted in her seat, and looking away from Rett, glanced out her window, this time actually seeing beyond the glass. She frowned to note they were on the far side of El Cajon. She hadn't thought anything of it when Rett headed east on 8, but this was farther out than a mere ride to sooth Ryann into sleep.

"Where are we going?"

"Sunday dinner."

"At Gram's?" No, no, no. Skye wasn't ready to deal with the Sullivan family en masse.

"Yeah. I was going to skip it today because Ryann was so upset. But when you suggested taking a ride, I realized family is what we both needed. I can tell everyone at the same time."

"Tell them? Tell them what?"

"That Ryann is my daughter."

"You haven't told them?" Appalled, Skye could only think this was not the time for an outsider to join the family for Sunday dinner.

"There was no reason to tell them before, and no opportunity since Cassie's death." He glanced at her and then back to the road, a half smile curling up the corner of his mouth. "Don't worry, there's always plenty to go around."

"Prepare yourself," Rett warned her with a wink a short while later and pushed the door open.

Drawing in a bracing breath, Skye followed him into a room exploding with people. Men, women, kids and one diminutive gray-haired lady fell on Rett as if they hadn't seen him in ages rather than days.

The Sullivans, en masse.

Rett had five brothers including his twin, all married, and from the number of toddlers and babies, all procreating. It looked like the whole family had come for Sunday dinner. The enticing scent of Italian food floated on the air.

"Skye." Rett's twin Rick was the first to spot her. He walked straight to her, shifted the baby he carried to one side and wrapped her in a huge hug. "How are you doing? I'm so sorry I wasn't able to make Aidan's funeral."

And the timing of that just struck Skye. The Sullivans hadn't made the services for Aidan and she'd understood because she knew they were all in Europe for the opening of the new international store. But Rett had been there. He'd given up the opening and the hundred-year anniversary celebration to be at the funeral.

Damn him. That mattered.

"I received the flowers and your card. Cassie appreciated your generosity."

He waved that aside. "I can't believe we've lost her, too. She was so young, it's such a loss."

"It is. She never got over losing Aidan. In the end she just stopped fighting."

He scowled and, though heavier and more conservative in style than Rett, suddenly looked just like his brother. "That's not right. She should have been thinking about Ryann."

"Yes," Skye agreed. Cassie had been her friend, but she'd left her child defenseless. Skye found that hard to forgive.

"Rick." A lovely woman with warm green eyes and dark red hair stepped up to him and hooked her arm through his. He greeted her with a kiss.

"You remember my wife, Savannah?"

"Yes, we met at Gram's birthday bash last year," Skye said. "I can't believe how big the family has gotten." The brothers had all been bachelors when she'd returned to San Diego six years ago.

"I know. It's out of control." Rick grinned. "But we're happy. You need to come in, meet everyone." He lifted the baby he held and turned him to face Skye. "This is my son, Joey."

"He's beautiful." The boy looked to be about a year old and had the same dark hair and straight brows as his dad and uncle Rett. A real cutie, he was a chubby little cherub. Skye quickly saw the similarity between him and Ryann.

It struck her suddenly that Ryann was a part of this huge family that still believed in Sunday dinners. Skye should feel happy for Ryann, and she did; but at the same time she'd never felt more alone.

Sometimes the lonely cost of protecting her heart came at too high a price.

"Excuse me." Suddenly overwhelmed, she made her excuses and headed for the door, looking for air and solitude. She only got a few feet before another brother snagged her and made new introductions. When it happened for the third time, she forced herself to relax and just go with it.

She'd grown up with these guys. Her father was the master jeweler for Sullivans' Jewels for twenty-eight years. She lost her mother around the same time the Sullivans lost their parents. Gram began bringing Rett and Rick into the store on weekends and her dad toted her and Aidan along as well. Together they'd run wild in the back halls of the jewelry store. On other occasions they'd run wild with the rest of the Sullivans here on Gram's estate in Paradise Pines.

Ford, the youngest Sullivan brother, was showing off his four-year-old twins when Rett strolled by and handed Skye an orange soda. She looked from the drink to his back. Had he remembered it was her favorite or had it been a random selection?

It irked her that she always seemed to know exactly where he was. The man had practically kidnapped her. To keep from tracking his movements she deliberately put her back to him.

"Skye Miller, come here, child." Matilda "Gram" Sullivan drew Skye into a comforting embrace to offer her condolences.

"It's good to see you, Gram." Tears choked Skye. This woman was the closest thing to a grandmother Skye had ever known. For just a moment she closed her eyes, held on tight and drew in the familiar scent of Chantilly.

"Come sit with me." The older woman drew Skye over to the couch and patted the spot next to her. "What you did was very naughty, but we're happy to have you back with us. You must tell me what you're doing these days. I hear you're a photographer. I'm not at all surprised. You always had a camera in your hands."

Skye sat and talked about her portrait and wedding photography business, but after a few minutes she challenged Gram's odd statement.

"Exactly what did I do that was so naughty?"

Gram tilted her head and contemplated Skye with somber eyes. "I don't know what happened between you and Rett all those years ago, but he changed after you left."

"What do mean?" Her gaze found Rett sitting at the

dining room table with his brothers Ford and Alex and a handful of kids. Rett was pale but smiling as he shoveled a spoonful of peaches into Ryann's mouth.

For all her friendliness, Gram's expression turned censuring. "Dear, you broke his heart."

"Are you sure you want to do this? Raising a kid is a lot of work." Holding his sleeping one-year-old, Rick leaned back against the white railing on the front porch.

"She's my daughter, of course I'm sure."

"Do you even know what you're getting yourself into? Babies are messy, hungry and loud. They're helpless, dependent and demanding. They cry when they're tired, when they want up, when they want down, when they're hurt, or unhappy or just because." Joey scrunched up his feet and moved his head to the other side on Rick's shoulder. Rick gently patted his son's back until he settled down.

Rick lowered his voice when he continued. "It's up to you to figure out what's wrong. This young she won't be able to tell you and that hurts, man. And she's still in diapers. Don't even get me started on poop."

"You're kidding me, right?" Rett nailed his twin with a hard stare. "You dote on that boy."

"Hey, I'm giving it to you real." Rick defended his rant. "Loving them is the easy part, comes without even trying. The thing you need to know about the loving part is it's huge, bigger than anything you'll ever know. That is kind of scary, but you know, in a good way. It's why you're willing to go through the whole care and feeding part."

"She's my daughter." Rett crossed his arms over his chest. "Duty demands I provide care and feeding."

Rick nodded his head toward the end of the porch and Skye, who sat talking to Jesse and Savannah.

Rett followed Rick's gaze. "It's a difficult time for Skye. She's struggling. And the alternative was foster care. Do you think I could do that? Just hand Ryann off as if I had no part in her conception?"

"You already did—"

Rett narrowed his eyes, slicing his brother with an icy glare.

Rick held up a placating hand.

"I know that's the place of a donor. Wasn't I right there drawing straws with you when Aidan approached us for help? I'm just saying you already made that emotional adjustment and Skye—"

"So I should just dismiss any obligation I have to Ryann?" Rett's chest felt tight at the very idea. He didn't know the baby well, yet. Somehow it had been awkward to spend much time with her while Aidan and Cassie were alive. Too complicated. And these were hardly ideal circumstances, but he already felt a connection to her.

"Parenting is hard work when you have the woman you love standing next to you," Rick advised. "It's going to be brutal on your own."

"And I'm too much of a wimp to handle it?"

"Man, you're taking this all wrong. No one is tougher

than you, more dogged—but this is going to change your life forever. Skye may be struggling but she'd be a good mother. You don't have to do this."

"You didn't have to marry Savannah when she got pregnant, either. But you freaked out when she turned you down."

"That's different. I loved Savannah."

"Not at the time."

"So you're saying that you still have feelings for Skye?"

"What? No." Rett actually took a step back. "Anything between us ended fifteen years ago."

"I thought you were going to give her a call after Aidan's funeral."

"Yeah, well, she didn't return my calls. Proof positive whatever we had is in the past." Hands stuffed into his pockets, Rett stared at the other end of the porch where Skye sat on a swing chatting with his sisters-in-law.

A breeze lifted the edges of her short, dark hair and she arched her neck to allow the air to caress her skin. She used to be such a sensual creature. Every move she made revealing her joy in her surroundings. Not anymore. Now she was locked up tighter than a chastity belt.

"You are so gone on her." Rick smirked.

Rett glared at his twin. He never used to smirk. Must be Savannah's influence.

"We're not having this conversation. And I'm not giving my daughter away. I can't believe you'd even suggest it. I didn't plan to raise Ryann, but now she needs me and I'm going to be there for her. Alex got custody of Gabe. Ford is raising twins that aren't his. Brock married Jesse when she was pregnant with another man's child. It's practically a family tradition."

Hurt by his twin's persistent questions, Rett rocked on his heels. Excited shouts and infectious laughter floated to him from the yard where little Sullivans frolicked in fun. Ford's twins were pulling Ryann and Alex's youngest across the lawn in a wagon. It did his heart good to see her laughing.

Rick clapped him on the shoulder. "There's not a thing you can't do if you put your mind to it. I'm just pointing out you have options here. Raising Ryann is going to change your life. You have an active social life, bachelor digs, a sports car. All of which will disappear once Ryann's settled in. Are you ready for that?"

Rett brooded over Rick's question. Everyone acted as if he hadn't thought the situation through, that because he was a bachelor he wouldn't be able to adjust. The truth was he'd considered all this before he agreed to act as Aidan and Cassie's donor. And this was the only eventuality that worked for him.

His daughter, his responsibility. His future.

But Rick's lack of faith shook him.

"You don't think I can do it?"

"Hell, yeah, I think you can," Rick said with feeling. "She's your daughter. What are you some kind of chump?"

"Now there's the brother I know and love." Relieved to have the world righted, Rett held out his hand and the brothers bumped knuckles. "You're the chump. Why are you busting my chops?" And then it hit him. "Skye."

"Yeah." Rick had the grace to look sympathetic. "You know I've always felt bad about the timing of my breakup, and yours and Skye's all those years ago."

"No one blames you for anything from fifteen years ago. There's no need for you to feel bad about anything."

"She broke you up. I don't want to see that happen again."

"We were kids. We're different people now."

"So you're ready to tell the family?"

Rett nodded. The time had come.

"Grab your girl then." Rick hefted Joey to his other shoulder. "I'll go gather the troops and meet you in the living room."

All important announcements took place in Gram's formal living room.

Rett walked down the steps and across the lawn to pick up Ryann. To the accompaniment of wails and protests, he herded the other kids toward the house where their mothers directed them inside.

Tense as one of the newel posts, Skye stood at the top of the steps, blocking his return, her maple-brown eyes carefully shielded.

"Good luck."

"You're not coming in?"

She shook her head. "It's a family thing."

He climbed up, and she carefully stepped aside. He followed, crowding her. "I want you beside me."

"Skye, pretty." Ryann patted Skye's cheek.

"Ryann's prettier." Skye's brown eyes dimmed with anguish before she squeezed them closed. When she opened them a new vulnerability shone through. She pressed Ryann's tiny hand to her cheek and turned to kiss the palm. "You're having fun, aren't you?"

"Wagon." Ryann pointed to the red plastic vehicle. "Ride.

"You want more rides?" Rett asked.

Ryann nodded.

"You got it," he promised. "As soon as we tell everyone you're the newest member of the family, we'll come back out and give you another ride."

Ryann nodded again and smiled shyly.

Rett shifted his gaze to Skye. "This was a good idea. Exactly what she needed. A little fun and a whole lot of distraction."

Tears welled up in Skye's eyes as she bit her lip. "Being with her cousins is helping her."

From the choked quality of her voice he could tell the admission cost her. No matter how she protested, she cared about Ryann.

Walking to the door with Ryann in his arms, Rett stopped when he reached the threshold to look back at Skye. He held out his hand.

"Please?"

CHAPTER FOUR

BACK IN SAN DIEGO Skye pulled the EXT into Rett's driveway and glanced at the man dozing slumped against the passenger door. Tapped out, he'd asked her to drive them home. And really, how could she refuse?

"Rett, wake up." She shook his arm. "We're home." She heard the words and immediately corrected herself. "You're home."

Rett coughed, a rough hacking from deep in his chest. By the end of the evening he'd been hoarse. Without opening his eyes he rolled his head on the back of the seat as if seeking a more comfortable resting spot. He radiated a heat she felt clear across the console.

"Come on." She gave him another shake. "Time to get you inside." When he still didn't move, she tried a different tact. "Rett, wake up. I need your help getting Ryann inside."

A scowl shadowed his brow before a deep sigh lifted his chest. His eyes opened and he leaned forward to scrub both hands over his face.

"Okay." He yawned. "Let's do this."

Glad to have him on the move, Skye grabbed her

purse and the diaper bag, removed the keys from the ignition and slid from the truck. Rett had Ryann out of her seat and propped on his shoulder so Skye led the way to the front door, using his keys to let them in.

In his bedroom, he put Ryann in a portable crib before flinging himself facedown on the king-size bed.

"Seriously?" Skye stood hands on her hips surveying man and baby, trying to determine which way to go first. The baby, she decided. Digging into the suitcase beside the crib, she pulled out pretty pink pajamas.

Exhausted both emotionally and physically, Ryann slept through the whole process of being changed, swabbed, powdered and pj'd, which made it fast and painless for both of them.

Once she had the baby ready for bed, Skye savored the bittersweet joy of having Ryann alone for the first time that day. Already she felt her guard slipping, but she couldn't resist the stolen opportunity to just hold the baby for a moment, rocking her gently, watching the slow rise and fall of her chest, taking in the sweet scent of baby and powder. Relishing the slight weight in her arms.

This was life, so precious, so fragile. Skye felt the need to guard Ryann's every breath. The baby gained so much with Rett's recognition today: family, status and security. And Skye wanted all of that for her niece. But it also left her feeling very alone.

She needed to stick to her plan, help father and daughter bond. Unfortunately, that meant setting her defenses—and her attitude—aside to try to work with the man. Who she noticed had stripped his shirt off again.

With a sigh, she placed Ryann in the portable crib and covered her with a warm blanket before turning to the man on the bed. A hand on his forehead confirmed his fever had returned. He moaned and turned into her cool touch.

"You need more medicine," she said more to herself than him.

Looking around the master suite, she took in the decor for the first time. Like the other rooms in the house, comfort and color played big parts. She admired the straight lines of the platform bed and the lush fabrics in gray, silver and black offset by a deep crimson. The bold and sexy room fit Rett.

Okay, she really didn't want to have sexy thoughts about Rett in his bedroom, so she forced her mind back to the task at hand. First she checked the bedside table and then the bathroom where she found the over-the-counter medicine.

In search of a glass she made her way down the hall and stepped up into the open kitchen. She drew a glass of water and decided to check the refrigerator, which was surprisingly full, for some type of juice. He had orange juice and she poured a large glass, of that, too.

Look at her being all domestic. But she justified her actions by reminding herself it was only because he needed to be healthy to take care of Ryann.

She carried the liquids back to his room where a light snore indicated Rett dozed. He'd rolled onto his back. A flush colored his cheeks under the five-o'clock shadow, but not even an illness detracted from his sheer maleness.

Driven to touch him, she brushed the hair off his forehead, thinking at one time he'd meant the world to her. He still had the power to quicken her pulse. His skin felt hot and dry, a reminder he needed the medicine to bring his temperature down.

"Rett," she said, giving his shoulder a good shake, and then another.

Finally he opened his eyes, blinked at her.

"Skye." Pure joy lit up his glassy gaze and a large hand hooked around her neck and pulled her down to him for a hot kiss.

Shock held her immobile while he deepened the caress, pushing past the line of her lips to tangle his tongue with hers. Caught in the heat of the moment she melted into the pleasure and familiarity of the embrace.

The long emotional day disappeared as she surrendered thought to sensation. Rett made her feel like a desirable woman. Rolling with her, he buried his hand in her hair, angling her head to deepen the kiss. Her blood simmered and she arched into him, ready to succumb to his sensual demand.

But self-preservation finally kicked in. Somehow she mustered the strength to pull free of his hold. She rolled to the side of the bed and scrambled to her feet.

"I can't do this." She swept her hair back with both hands and then tugged at the hem of her shirt.

He scowled and blinked at her, then awareness sharpened his expression.

"Are you still here?" He pushed himself into a half upright position.

"I brought your medicine." She gestured to the bedside table while stepping back, trying to make her retreat appear dignified when in fact she was scurrying to get out of his reach.

She just kept herself from wiping her mouth. Not that he tasted bad, totally not the problem. But she'd fought too hard to put the memory of him behind her to let the feel and taste of him derail her now.

She was stronger and smarter these days; emotion no longer ruled her.

"I put Ryann down," she said more to break the silence than for any other reason.

He scrubbed both hands over his face, and then swung both feet to the floor. Tossing a couple of the pills to the back of his throat, he swallowed them with half the water.

"Thank you," he said, reaching for the orange juice, "for everything."

She stood in silence while he drank, steeling herself to be patient when every atom in her demanded she leave. Now. Then she realized there was nothing keeping her here.

"Yeah, I hope you feel better. I gotta go."

She immediately wished the words back when he pushed the blanket aside and sat up.

Despite her best efforts, her gaze strayed to his bare

chest, roughened with hair narrowing down to the waistband of his low riding jeans.

Drawing her eyes away from all that bronzed skin, she noticed he'd nearly finished the orange juice. She was just thinking his color looked better when he looked up, piercing her with his blue eyes.

"Will you stay the night?"

Skye set her purse on the table beside Rett's bed. She was such a sucker. She should be at home in her small apartment in Mira Mesa, but of course she agreed to stay and help out.

When he said he was worried he wouldn't hear Ryann if she woke in the night, Skye had felt she had no choice. The fact he'd asked spoke for itself.

And if her heart quickened and her body heated before he explained himself, she preferred to play ignorant.

He'd taken himself off to the guest room, which was apparently downstairs and out of earshot of the master bedroom. That meant Skye would be sleeping in Rett's bed, something she never thought she'd willingly do again.

On autopilot, she opened the sliding glass door to the terrace, letting the night breeze in to air out the room.

Seeking a distraction, her thoughts bounced back to Gram's comment from earlier that day. It had been nagging at Skye for hours.

She broke Rett's heart?

Now there was a fictional rewriting of history if she'd ever heard one.

But why would Gram make up such a thing?

She wouldn't, of course.

Much as Skye longed to dismiss the statement as total nonsense she knew Gram well enough to know she wouldn't say it if she didn't believe it. Which meant either Rett had played the wounded lover or he'd been more affected by the breakup than she thought.

The first didn't sound like Rett. A lack of tolerance for liars and bull excrement was something they'd had in common. So did that mean Gram had been right?

Grabbing up the T-shirt Rett lent her to sleep in, Skye headed into the bathroom, checking on Ryann en route. As she stepped into the shower, the conversation with Gram ran through her head.

"Oh, Gram, I think you're mistaken," she'd protested. "I didn't have the power to break his heart."

"Child, I may not know the details, but I know heartache when I see it. Hard to miss when two people you love are suffering right in front of you."

"Two people?" she asked trying to get a handle on the conversation and her emotions.

"Yes, Rick's engagement broke up right at that same time. I remember he came home one weekend, announced it was over and he was going hiking for a couple of days to get his head around it. I was worried about him going alone, but Rett showed up to go with him, said he had things of his own to think about."

If Rett went hiking up Mount Laguna that summer,

it explained why Skye hadn't been able to reach him. Reception in the mountains was spotty at the best of times. Fifteen years ago it would have been nonexistent.

"So he was upset before he went away that weekend?" The question slipped out.

Gram shook her head. "Not Rett. He was more thoughtful than upset. I got the feeling he wanted to tell me something, but decided to hold off."

"It doesn't sound like he was heartbroken."

"Not yet. When they came back, Rick was subdued and headed straight into the city. Rett lingered a bit. He was excited, showed me some designs he'd drawn while he was out. They were beautiful, became the first of his signature series. But it was the ring that stood out, a bridal set with a magnificent round diamond in a tower of baguettes. It was lovely—"

"Gram—" Skye broke in needing to stop the picture she presented. "Please."

"Of course, I'm sorry." Gram patted her hand. "The point is Rett was excited when he left my place. After that, you were gone and he was heartsick for a long time. And the designs I mentioned? He made all of the pieces he'd drawn. Except the ring."

Okay, Skye conceded while brushing her teeth, maybe Rett hadn't been as unaffected by the circumstances of their breakup as she'd thought. But it didn't matter. Too much time had passed.

And when it came to memories, Skye didn't have to dig too deep to recall Rett's halfhearted-duty-inspired proposal. His reaction to the news she was pregnant had hurt, but she hadn't doubted it was honest.

And rehashing it wouldn't change anything. Nothing positive anyway.

Okay, so now she knew where he'd disappeared to, and why; but, really, what difference did it make? Gram could romanticize the drawing of the ring; Skye knew it was just wishful thinking. If Rett had meant the ring for Skye, he never would have let her get on the plane and fly away.

She folded the towel and tucked it over the rail and then flipped out the light.

It might all have been different if there had been a reason for the miscarriage, a fall, an accident that jarred her, anything. But there'd been nothing. Her body had simply rejected the fetus, and the doctor said that was fairly common.

She'd worked very hard to put the loss of her lover behind her while coping with the miscarriage. Yes, she'd run, she'd felt alone, empty, inadequate. And Rett hadn't tried to stop her or come after her. That brought home the real tragedy, the loss of her best friend.

Those were bad times, an ugly place. She couldn't—wouldn't—be drawn back there.

Rett stumbled upstairs at eight the next morning craving coffee and a shower. He ran the backs of his fingers over his jaw, and a shave. Coughing, he pondered where to start.

Skye stood up from the couch. She was fully dressed, looking fresh and lovely. And a tad pinched.

"Good morning," he greeted her, his voice still hoarse from overuse the day before. "Thanks for staying last night."

She nodded. "Ryann is still sleeping." She rounded the sofa and headed for the door. "I suggest letting her sleep as long as possible. Hopefully she'll be more subdued when she's more rested. Call me if you need any help."

"Wait." She was leaving, but he wasn't ready for her to go. "Let me fix you some breakfast to show my appreciation."

"That's not necessary." She opened the door. "We're not buddies, Rett. I promised to help out with Ryann and I will. I just need a couple of days to get my head around all of this." With that she stepped outside and closed the door.

Rett shook his head and followed.

"Skye." He stopped her as she prepared to climb into her silver Camry. "You can't live life behind an icy wall without suffering from the cold. By hiding away you're only hurting yourself."

"Don't patronize me." She confronted him over the top of the car. "You bounce from woman to woman like you're on a trampoline. Never allowing yourself to stay with anyone long enough to build a relationship. You're just as afraid to care about someone as I am. At least I'm honest about it."

He rubbed his chest, stung by the accuracy of her barb. "You don't know what you're talking about."

She smiled sweetly.

"Oh, did I touch a nerve?" She opened her car door. "We're going to need someone to watch her during the day. Why don't you line up some interviews for Wednesday." She ducked into her car and drove away.

He watched her until she turned at the corner. He should be angry at her personal attack, but he recognized desperation when he saw it. Skye had lost everyone she loved. And she was afraid to risk her heart again.

He made his way back into the house, checked on Ryann, who still slept. With her dark hair and creamy white, petal soft skin she looked so much like Skye. After his and Skye's conversation last night, looking at Ryann wrenched something inside him, made him wonder what their child would have looked like. He'd had to put the thought of the miscarriage, the loss of his child, aside years ago or it would have driven him slowly crazy.

He'd learned dwelling on the past never accomplished anything, so he shook the painful notion aside and stepped into the shower.

Ten minutes later he strolled into the kitchen ready for coffee only to find it already brewed. A glass of orange juice sat on the island counter along with a dose of his cold medicine.

Skye may talk tough but she had a marshmallow center. Which was exactly what he was counting on.

CHAPTER FIVE

"WHAT IS the youngest child you've worked with?" Skye asked the attractive young woman sitting across from her and Rett in his living room Wednesday afternoon. This was their third interview of the day. The first two had been dismissed and Skye was not hopeful with this one, either. She already had the sense the woman's IQ may be exceeded by her bra size.

"A four-year-old." The woman responded though not to Skye, her attention never wavered from Rett. She crossed her legs so her short red skirt inched farther up her bare thighs. "That was a couple of years ago. My last assignment the children were seven and nine."

"So." Skye checked the paperwork on the table. "Alessia, you have no experience with a one-year-old?"

"Two," Rett inserted. "She's almost two."

"She looks so sweet." The woman twisted her hair around a finger. "I'm sure I'll be able to handle her with no problem."

Skye snorted. The woman hadn't even glanced at Ryann who quietly played with blocks on the floor at Rett's feet. Skye flicked her glance to Rett. He hadn't asked a single question. Lounging back on the couch, the corner of his sensual mouth turned up as his gaze roamed over the prospective nanny.

"Did you get along well with both children?"

"The little girl was a doll. She liked to please, so she was easy. The little boy was a br—more challenging. He took joy in arguing."

Skye looked to see if Rett had noticed the near slip. He'd leaned forward and appeared to be paying more attention.

"And how did you handle that?"

Alessia shrugged. "He spent a lot of time in time-out."

"Is that your preferred method of discipline?" Finally a question from Rett.

"Their parents didn't believe in spanking."

"Exactly why did you leave your last assignment?" Skye probed.

Alessia rolled her eyes. "Their mother had a new man in her life and she didn't like the way he looked at me, so she told me my services were no longer needed."

"I think I've heard all I need to." Skye pasted on a smile and stood. "Please excuse us for a moment. Rett."

She strode into the kitchen, turned to wait for Rett, saw the flirtatious smile Alessia gave him. He lifted a brow in query as he came to lean against the counter.

"I like her."

Skye caught a lock of her hair and twisted it around her finger. "Oh, really?"

He grinned. "So she's friendly, you can't hold that against her."

"She's never worked with a child as young as Ryann. I vote no."

"Which doesn't mean she can't. She believes she can handle her." He glanced over at Alessia, got a little wave.

Aggravated, Skye flicked his ear.

"Ouch." Rett covered his ear but he gave her his attention. "That hurt."

"So does spanking."

"Yeah, I caught that. I vote no."

She narrowed her eyes at him. "You were messing with me."

His grin returned. "She lost me at brat."

"Ha ha." Skye flicked his other ear.

He laughed and grabbing her hand pulled her close to slant his mouth across hers. "She doesn't hold a candle to you."

Skye licked her lips as she stepped back, tasted him with the sweep of her tongue. "You have a better chance with her."

"Nah." He ran his thumb over the dip in her chin. "No challenge."

She shook her finger at him. "Don't do that again." He eyed her finger and she pulled it out of his reach. "So we keep looking?"

"Oh, yeah."

Rolling her eyes at him, Skye went to tell Alessia her services wouldn't be needed.

Rett watched the subtle sway of her hips surprisingly emphasized by her no-nonsense stride. Rubbing his ear, he grinned. He did enjoy messing with her. She rose so beautifully to the bait.

What he didn't enjoy was feeling the sting himself.

After seeing her at Aidan's funeral, so brave and strong, yet so alone, he'd called her thinking she'd need someone. That's what he told himself; it was just to stay in touch with an old friend.

Right. She hadn't been in his house for more than a few hours and he had her in his arms drinking in the taste of her. Lord, she felt so good, so familiar it had felt like coming home.

And now here he was kissing her some more, messing with her. When he knew in his soul she was the one who could mess him up good. He had to stop. Because no matter how easy it was falling into old ways, no one had the power to hurt him like Skye.

On Friday, at a rare weeknight wedding, Skye lined up a shot through her camera.

The bride and groom were at the cake table preparing to cut the cake. No announcement had been made yet so the only ones gathered were three of the bride's young nieces and nephew, the oldest of which was no more than two years old. Skye snapped several shots knowing the bride would appreciate the pictures as much as the traditional shots of the feeding of the cake.

She'd already taken the formal photos of the cake, a lavish affair of swirls, beading and roses in white and pink topped by dual crystal hearts set in a bower of baby roses. The DJ announced the cutting of the cake and Skye held her ground as friends and family gathered around.

She framed the shot. The bride was stunning in a strapless sheath dress and the groom looked more relaxed in his shirtsleeves, though the bow tie was still snug at his neck.

"Come on, Tina, give it to him good," a good-natured voice called.

In spite of several calls for more action the couple were playful but respectful as they fed the first bite to each other.

These were the last of her assigned shots. She'd stick around for a while, get some candids of the dancing and then she'd be free to join the party or leave. As she rarely knew any of the guests, she usually chose to leave.

"You were always a bit of a romantic. It's no wonder you ended up a wedding photographer."

Rett.

How did she get so lucky? She hadn't seen him in the crowd, but then her major focus was the bride and groom. With a sigh she lowered her camera and turned to face him.

"Not such a romantic anymore." Just the sight of him brought the hard press of his mouth against hers to mind.

She licked her lips. Before this week, fifteen years had passed since he last kissed her. Yet when his lips claimed hers it was like no time had passed at all. And oh he knew how to use his mouth.

"No? I hear you're very good."

"I am. Who has Ryann?"

"I knew you cared. She's with Rick and Savannah." The music started in again. He held out a hand. "Dance with me."

"I'm working."

"Take a break."

"What about your date?"

He lifted a dark brow. "What about her?"

"Won't she have a problem with you dancing with another woman?"

His eyes mocked her. "It's not that kind of relationship. And it's only a dance."

Not waiting for further arguments he stopped a passing waiter and relieving her of her camera, he set it on the waiter's tray along with a twenty-dollar bill. "Stand here and watch this for a few minutes."

"Wait—"

"No." He clasped her hand and drew her on to the dance floor where he pulled her confidently into his arms.

Protocol demanded women not outshine the bride, but there was no mention of the groom. Good thing. Rett in a dark Armani suit, stark white shirt and custom tie delegated every other man in the room to the background. Moreover, it hid a body hard with muscle.

"How's Ryann doing at the day care?" Instead of a full-time nanny they'd chosen to go with an option

Jesse suggested. She had her kids in the Rise and Shine Preschool and raved about how good they were. "Does she still like it?"

"Loves it. And Gwen is working out great." Rick and Savannah's housekeeper had recommended her sister to them. She did housekeeping and some child care. "It's good to be back at work."

"I imagine."

"I meant to tell you, a gal from Child Services stopped by yesterday. Talked to me, and Gwen, and spent some time with Ryann. She seemed nice enough, said she'd be contacting you."

"She hasn't called me."

"She didn't call, just showed up."

"Great. Did she say anything about Ryann sleeping in your room? You really need to set her up in a room of her own."

"She didn't say anything. And it's only been a week, but I get it. Can you take her on Monday? Remember Gwen told us she'd need it off when she started. I really have to finish a commission that's due."

Skye chewed her lip, and then nodded. It really was her turn.

"You ran off before I could thank you properly last Monday. I truly did appreciate your help."

"I didn't do it for you. I did it for Ryann."

"Do you regret coming to my rescue?" he asked, his voice low and husky. "I was glad to have you with me."

"Give me a break. Except for your grand announcement,

you spent the day chatting up your brothers and playing Clue."

"Hey, Clue is a game that requires mental acuity. I was sick." He led her in an expert turn. "They took advantage of me."

"Good for them."

"Ouch. That's harsh."

"You deserve it." Curiously she felt the tension ease away as she gave him a hard time. "It was a tough day for me. I say kudos to whoever took you down."

"Vindictive. That's new." His gaze ran over her. "I like it."

"I'm not eighteen anymore, Rett."

"We're both older and wiser." A sigh stirred the hair at her nape. "Have you come to terms with the fact I'm Ryann's father?"

"Not really, no." How could he expect her to understand when they'd come so close to having a child together? Her arms had been empty for fifteen years yet he just gave his baby away.

Okay that was unfair, but she couldn't help the way she felt.

In her head she understood he'd done a very generous and self-sacrificing thing by acting as a donor for her brother and sister-in-law, but her heart ached for the past. If he'd had a different reaction to her pregnancy, they might still be together today, and she'd be the mother of his children.

Not that she could ever say any of that aloud so instead she said, "It was good seeing your grandmother."

"Yeah, I saw you talking to Gram."

"She looks great. And she's still as sharp as ever."

"That's Gram." He agreed, his pride and affection clear.

"She accused me of breaking your heart." Now why did she say that? There was no point in bringing it up but to embarrass herself.

Silence blared between them as the music swelled and he spun her in a series of tight circles. Skye gritted her teeth and hung on.

"Yeah, well, there are some things you can't hide from someone who knows you back to your diapers."

"What?" She snapped her head up, scanned his profile for clues to his motives. "Now you're saying I broke your heart?"

"I'm not saying anything. This is your conversational bent, not mine."

"This is ridiculous. There must be a dimensional time warp here in California because history has been rewritten in San Diego."

"I remember our history just fine."

"Then you should remember you were the one who walked away from me."

"I remember you asked for time to think, so I left you alone for a few days. When I came back, you'd lost the baby and were hopping a plane east."

"I tried to get a hold of you for two days. You didn't return a single call." She wondered if he'd explain where he'd been, if he'd confirm Gram's version of that summer.

"I was hiking the mountains helping Rick work out some things and doing some thinking of my own. It was quite a bomb you dropped on me."

So Gram had been right. But he was still defensive. And she so wasn't going through this again.

"It didn't matter in the end anyway. I lost the baby."

"And I was sorry about that."

"Yeah, I remember how eager you were to be a father." She cringed at the bitterness ripe in her voice.

He didn't respond for a minute and when he did, he quietly, sincerely repeated himself. "I was sorry when you lost the baby. Sorry I wasn't there to help you through the miscarriage. But it was you who left me. You who got on a plane and flew away. I've always been right here. And I'm going to be right here for my daughter."

"Oh, God. Don't call her that." Skye squeezed her eyes shut, felt tears wet her cheeks. She bowed her head, hiding them from him.

"I don't know what else to call her."

"She's my niece." Though they both knew she wasn't. "Or are you going to pretend Aidan and Cassie had no part in her creation?"

"Skye." She heard his aggravation. "It would be different if they'd lived. But they're gone and this isn't easy for any of us."

"Oh, God. You're not going to tell her." Skye felt her link to her brother slipping further and further away.

"I will. When she's older, I'll explain everything. But the reality is I'm her father."

Yes, that fact had been hammered home. Thank God the music had ended. Without looking at him, she pulled free of his hold. "I've got to go."

Skye sat at the desk in the corner of her living room and worked on the pictures from the wedding where she'd danced with Rett. Turns out she had caught him in a shot of the crowd at the reception. He sat with a voluptuous redhead. She clung to his arm and whispered in his ear. He gazed at her with indulgence.

Everything about her was focused on him, but he'd said they didn't have an exclusive relationship.

Telling herself it was none of her business, Skye deliberately moved to the next picture, blocking out any personal emotions.

She really tried to tell a story with her presentation. Each wedding was the embodiment of a bride's biggest fantasy, and Skye did her best to recreate the emotional journey in pictures. It really had been a beautiful wedding. The event planner enhancing the bride's choice of pink and silver with crystals, pearls and mirrors for a venue that sparkled with opulent elegance.

Carefully choosing borders and music she unfolded the day into three parts: prep, wedding and reception. And using candids intermixed with formal shots to create a cohesive story.

Pleased with her results, she saved her work and closed down her computer. She got up for a soda and stopped to flip though her mail. A letter from her apartment complex caught her attention. A quick read revealed a new owner was converting the apartments to condos. She had sixty days to move from the premises. As a current tenant, she was invited to make a bid on her unit as soon as the renovations were complete.

Skye slowly sank onto the stool at her counter and gave a disbelieving laugh. She was losing her home. What more could go wrong?

"Please, God, send me something good for a change."

A knock sounded at her door. Seeing Rett through the peephole made her wonder if the universe were playing games with her.

Because no way was Rett an answer to her prayers.

What could he want? It galled her to do it, because really he meant nothing to her, but she stepped back to the hall mirror to check her appearance. She fluffed fingers through her short hair and licked her lips to give them a little sheen.

Finally she rolled her eyes and went to answer the door.

"Rett." She leaned against the door frame. "What are you doing here? Where's Ryann?"

He nodded toward the street where his big, black EXT was double-parked.

"She's a little fussy tonight and wondered if you'd like to take a ride with us."

"She?"

His eyes flashed but he inclined his head. "Okay, we wondered if you'd like to take a ride with us?"

She hesitated. But the thought of Ryann in distress got to her.

"Let me grab my jacket."

"I'll meet you at the truck."

It took only a minute to slide into her shoes, pull on her jacket and grab her wallet and keys.

The brisk November air stung her cheeks as she trotted to where Rett stood beside the open door to the big vehicle.

She heard Ryann crying as she got closer.

"I guess she's having a bad night?"

He ran a hand through tousled brown hair. "It's been one drama after another. But the problem is she's over-tired."

"Poor baby. I'm surprised she didn't fall asleep coming over here then."

"She's fighting it."

"Let me get in back with her. Maybe that'll settle her down."

He frowned, but opened the back door. "Whatever you think will help."

Skye climbed up into the truck and Rett closed her in. She strapped in and then turned her attention to the wailing girl.

"Hey, Ryann. How are you, baby?" It took a few minutes to penetrate her distress but Skye continued to talk quietly to her. When she heard change, she reached into her pocket and pulled out her keys, which held a mini flashlight. She played the light over Ryann's lap effectively distracting her.

First she tried to catch the moving light, giggling when it shifted so she could chase it again. And when she figured out it came from something Skye held, she wanted to do it herself.

Skye let her play and after a bit, she offered Ryann her juice cup. The girl grabbed it and started sipping. Moments later her eyes slid closed.

Skye felt like she'd crossed the finish line of a full throttle marathon. When the baby didn't stir after five minutes, Skye climbed into the front seat to join Rett.

"Silence is golden."

The glance he sent her was full of gratitude. "You are a miracle worker."

"What happened today?"

He shook his head. Ran a weary hand over the back of his neck.

"I had to work late on that commission I told you about. Ryann went home from day care with Jesse. She was having fun playing with her cousins. She didn't want to leave with me when I got there at six. Then she wouldn't eat. It went downhill from there."

"She's still adjusting."

"We're still adjusting."

"They say kids thrive on routine."

"Yeah, well, I'm trying." But frustration clearly ate at him.

"This is a big change for both of you," she pointed out gently. "It's going to take time. It's only been a couple of weeks."

"My life is never going to be the same." It was a statement.

"You're whining to the wrong person."

He glanced at her, reached out a hand that he let fall on the seat between them. "Sorry."

"You'll find your rhythm," she said to her window. "And when you do, your life will be better, fuller. You have a child. That's life's best gift ever."

"I know. Do you think I don't know that?"

"Then act like it."

"I'm here, aren't I?" he demanded. "Driving to no-where at ten o'clock at night."

"It was your schedule that got off, not hers."

"Sometimes that's going to happen."

"Exactly."

"Wait." He did a double take between her and the road. "What?"

She sighed. "My point is, give yourself a break. There are going to be good days and bad days. And you're doing your best. So stop beating yourself up."

He halted at a red light and gave her a long, unread-able look.

"You really feel that way?" he finally asked.

"I do. And it's not easy for me to admit."

He flashed her an appreciative glance before mov-ing forward with the green light. He shrugged and she saw some of the tension drop away from his shoulders.

"You've been very helpful. Thanks." He made a turn that would take them back toward her place. "How did you get her to stop crying?"

She flashed her light over the steering wheel. "Dis-traction is my tool of choice. I find it works ninety per-cent of the time."

"Yeah?" By his tone she knew he was making note of the comment. "What do you do the other ten percent of the time?"

"Feed her, change her. Wait her out. Her folks usually showed up before I got too desperate. Plus I didn't have her very often."

"These days her dad's the one that's desperate."

"You'll get so you're not. And don't sweat it that she didn't want to go with you. It happened to Cassie a couple of times when she picked Ryann up from my place. It's not about you so much as it's about the fun you're taking her away from."

A half laugh escaped him. "Well, that's a relief and humbling at the same time."

"With kids it's all about the moment they're in."

"Where'd you learn so much about kids?"

"Mostly watching Cassie with Ryann and my own time with her. I also do school pictures for a couple of local academies, kindergarten through fifth grade. I always throw the preschool poses in for free. That's a wild time I can tell you, but those teachers know what they're doing."

"Great. You were a lifesaver tonight."

"Actually you rescued me tonight. I've had quite a day, too. The child advocate came by as I was leaving this morning. I had to stop and go back inside, show her around. She tried to make it quick, but I was still late. And when you got there tonight, I was sulking over an eviction notice."

CHAPTER SIX

"YOU RECEIVED an eviction notice?" Skye's news slammed into Rett like a fist to the gut. Every protective impulse he possessed stood up and roared in protest. His hands fisted on the wheel. "You should have said something sooner. How much do you need to get out of the hole?"

"Oh, I don't need—"

"If you're being evicted, you need help."

She cocked her head and eyed him curiously. "You're angry."

"Yes. Damn it." He waved in the air between them. "We're friends. We grew up together. Okay, I realize we have a history, and haven't exactly been close these last few years, but you have to know you could come to me for help. And if not me, Rick. But no, you'd rather lose your home."

"Rett, stop." Her hand settled over the bare skin of his forearm and squeezed.

He stared at her delicate fingers against his darker, rougher skin. This was the first time she'd touched him of her own accord.

"It's okay. I'm not being evicted because I couldn't pay my rent. They're converting the apartments to condos."

"Oh." He narrowed his eyes at her. "So what's the deal here, Skye? You must have known how I would take that. Was this some kind of test?"

"No. I'm sorry." She shook her head, her dark hair shining even in the dim light of the dash. "That was just me being dramatic. I should have realized you'd immediately go into fix-it mode."

"You're putting this on me?"

"Of course not. I'm just saying my life has been one drama after another for the last year, and now I'm being evicted. It's too much."

"You're sure? You didn't get hit with any of the expenses for Aidan's or Cassie's services did you, because I'll see you get reimbursed from the estate."

"My finances are fine. I'm not helping you with Ryann to get my hands on her trust, if that's what you're worried about."

"Not going in the right direction if you want to offset the anger thing," Rett gritted out.

"Right." She returned her hand to her lap, turned to look out the window. "That was uncalled for. I'm not handling this very well. Thanks for your concern, but I can take care of myself."

"You can help me but I can't help you? Hardly seems fair."

"I prefer to rely on myself."

"Friends are usually considered a good thing."

She lifted a shoulder, let it drop. "I have friends."

"But none you rely on."

"Right."

"What happened to you, Skye? You used to be as open and light as your name. What happened to your joy?"

"I don't know." She cleared her throat, but a huskiness remained when she continued. "I guess everyone I've lost took a piece of it when they left."

"That's pretty sad. You know, don't you, that the old Skye would say you need new people in your life to build it back up again."

"Luckily I've grown older and wiser. Now, I know new people in your life just gives you someone else to lose."

Rett sipped his wine, relaxing for the first time in days as the bold flavors warmed his tongue. He'd needed this, a night out for himself.

The lights were dim, a rare steak sizzled on his plate and a beautiful blonde chatted about nothing important. Perfect. Not a fussy baby in sight.

Understanding Ryann's distress didn't make it any easier to deal with. His patience was stretched thin. Tonight was as much for her as for him. The sitter had assured him she could handle the situation.

He leaned back in his chair and smiled at his companion.

"You're quiet tonight." Cindy twirled her wineglass, not even glancing at the food in front of her.

"I enjoy listening to you." He enjoyed not having to think. And not having to make sense of baby talk. He cut into his steak, savored the bite. Though truthfully Ryann amazed him with how well she spoke on the rare occasions when she wasn't upset.

"Oh." Cindy's eyes lit up and she leaned forward, offering him a stunning view of her magnificent assets. But she must have sensed his preoccupation because she asked, "What did I say?"

He leaned forward, too, showing her his appreciation by running his gaze over her. "How could you possibly expect me to concentrate on anything except how lovely you look tonight?"

Her sultry eyes flashed. "Nice save." She played with his fingers. "But you're not completely here. I know we're not exclusive, Rett, but I do expect your attention when we're together."

He couldn't argue. Not that he'd explain. He hadn't told any of the women in his life about Ryann, and he didn't intend to. No need to complicate casual relationships with thoughts of babies.

"I'm sorry. Why don't we finish up here and go back to your place. I'll make it up to you."

Her smile revealed she liked that idea, but before she responded his phone rang.

Damn.

Cindy blinked. Understandable. He usually turned his phone off when on a date. Just another way Ryann had changed his life.

He pulled out the phone. Yep, it was the sitter.

"You're not going to answer that," she demanded.

"I have to." He pushed away from the table. "Excuse me."

As he walked away, he pressed the connect button. "Hi, Patty."

"I'm sorry to disturb you, Mr. Sullivan, but Ryann just keeps crying and crying. I can't get her to calm down."

"Have you tried putting on her favorite DVD?"

"I've tried everything. She just cries and calls for you."

"For me?" That surprised him. "You mean her mother."

"No, for you. And she keeps saying sky. Maybe she's afraid you went to heaven like her mom."

Ryann was asking for him. And Skye. He hadn't given the sitter Skye's number because she was working tonight. Something shifted inside him. He was disappointed his evening was over, but a different urgency consumed him.

"I'll be there in twenty minutes."

A week later Skye once again found herself on Rett's doorstep. It seemed like she spent more time at his place than her own these days. Today he asked for her help converting a room into a bedroom for Ryann.

She'd decided to be happy for the opportunity. Taking the view that this was a chance to push Rett and Ryann together; anything that helped father and daughter get close was a good thing.

Her getting closer to Rett, not so much.

She needed to be careful not to let his generosity and proximity get to her. She was already too emotional over the whole custody issue; she couldn't afford to let him get too close.

He'd proven to be strong, confident, compassionate; it would be so easy, too easy, to lean on him, to take comfort and a moment's peace from him. Or be distracted by the heat of him.

Beyond anything else she had to hold strong against the temptation of him, against them falling again.

Because the comfort and peace were illusions. She could only rely on herself.

But, oh my, his desire was a powerful weapon. The want in his eyes reached right to the core of her, made her pulse race and her heart flutter. Made her realize it had been too long since she'd felt feminine and achy, like a woman. Like a desirable woman.

Hitching her purse up on her shoulder, she knocked on the door.

When she moved back to San Diego six years ago, she broke off a casual relationship. She'd been involved with a couple of men in the past few years, but nothing that grew too serious. She fully knew she had trust issues.

After losing so many people in her life, she feared risking her heart again. Especially to someone who'd broken it in the past.

The door opened and Rett stood there looking good in khaki shorts and a brown T-shirt.

"Hey, come in." He stepped aside. "I appreciate your help. Ryann, look who's here."

Ryann stood playing with a toy piano on the coffee table. As soon as she saw Skye, her face lit up and she came running.

Skye swept the baby up into her arms. She swallowed hard as little arms wrapped around her neck and clung. Instinctively, Skye held Ryann tightly, careful not to squeeze too hard.

How was she supposed to resist such unrestrained joy at her appearance?

They'd spent a quiet day together last week. Since Cassie's death, Skye hadn't been able to grasp the level of detachment she needed from Ryann. The child's despondency touched Skye deeply. It was stronger than sympathy, more personal. They both knew how it felt to lose those most important to them.

Every time Skye saw Ryann it saddened her to think Ryann would never know Aidan—that he'd already been replaced in her life.

It was both a sad and happy fact that life went on. Not that it deadened the pain; it just buried it under time.

Ryann had lost the parents who wanted her so desperately and loved her wholeheartedly, but she'd gained a new and extensive family who welcomed her with open arms. But the same fate that gave her that boon stole the last of Skye's family from her. She was all alone except for the fragile legal link to the daughter of her brother's heart.

For Ryann the sorrow would be brief, at least for

now. She'd adjust and form new affections for Rett, Gram, her new aunts, uncles and cousins. But the time would come when she'd want her mother, when she'd long for that special confidante to help her find her way from girl to woman. Skye understood that instinctual yearning.

Here was why Cassie had thrown Skye together with Rett. She'd known Ryann would need a woman's presence in her life and Cassie had given her Skye knowing she, better than anyone else in Ryann's new life, would know what losing a mother meant to a child.

After a couple of minutes, she tried to set the baby down, but Ryann hung on to Skye refusing to put her feet down.

Giving up, she dropped her purse on the sofa, settled Ryann on her hip and turned to Rett.

"Have you decided on what room you're going to convert?"

"There's the guest suite downstairs."

She planted her free hand on her hip. "Rett, she's not quite two years old and you want to tuck her away clear across the house and downstairs? Not a wise decision."

He scratched his jaw. "You could be right about that."

She rolled her eyes; he was such a guy. She headed down the hall. "You're going to have to give up one of your playrooms. Which is it going to be, the gym or the media room?"

"Why not the office?" He trailed behind her, checking out the rooms as if seeing them for the first time.

"I assumed you used it for business."

"I design and make jewelry. I use the workshop for business."

"So you don't care which of the other rooms we convert?"

"I didn't say that. It's a tough choice. I use the gym and media room most days." Hands in his pockets, he turned in a circle contemplating his choices. "But I use the computer a lot, too."

"You can move the desk with your computer into the workshop or the media room." She suggested. "Or your bedroom for that matter. Or you could move the function of one of these rooms down to the guest suite."

"Actually the guest room gets quite a bit of activity from the family, or it used to. But moving the desk is a good idea. In fact, we could move anything. Which room would you choose for Ryann?"

"Hmm." Pleased he'd asked for her opinion, Skye strolled to his bedroom doorway and turned back to approach the rooms from his end of the hall. The office was the closest and opened off to the right, which put it at the back of the house. The first room on the left was a bathroom and then came the gym followed by the media room, both at the front of the house.

She paused inside the media room. Decorated in gray and red a plump U-shaped sectional faced a huge flat screen TV. She smiled at the old-fashioned popcorn machine in the corner. No, she couldn't see the desk fitting in here.

"You have a TV in your room, in the living room and in the kitchen. Do you really need a TV room, too?"

"There's one down in the game room, too. And in the guest suite. I like TVs and I like to be able to see what I'm watching wherever I go in the house."

Yeah, she remembered he'd always had a TV going in the apartment he'd shared with Rick all those years ago. Rick complained about the racket, but Rett said he liked the noise, that it reminded him of home.

"Can I see the space downstairs?"

"Sure." He led the way to a huge, open room furnished with a large pool table, a poker table, a couple of club chairs and another extreme TV. A wall of windows overlooked a yard lush with plants and grass and a cool blue swimming pool.

At the far end of the room a lovely bar area, complete with a granite counter, full-size refrigerator and microwave, was framed by two doors. One led into a dream bath that had a walk-in glass shower, a hot tub under a skylight and a sauna.

"This is fabulous. No wonder the guest suite gets a lot of action if they have access to all this," she said as she ran her hand over the bronze granite countertop.

"The guest suite has its own bath."

She sent him an arch look. "Well, of course. This is a lot of house for one person. The downstairs alone is bigger than my whole apartment."

"Now you know why I like the TVs. They keep me company."

Shades of the past. "Are you lonely, Rett?"

"What? Are you kidding me? With my family? You

remember them? Five brothers. My twin. And don't forget Gram."

Ryann squirmed so Skye set her down. The little girl ran across the room giggling at the sound of her Mary Jane's clicking on the hardwood floor.

"I know how close you all are," Skye agreed as she strolled to the other door and peeked inside the guest room. Done in white and green, it looked like a hotel room in an upscale spa. The coverlet on the bed was so white and fluffy it would be like sleeping on a cloud.

She turned back to Rett. "I also know your brothers are all married now."

"Which only means I have five sisters to add to the mix." He walked over to the pool table, sent a ball rolling over the burgundy felt. "They're all great ladies."

"Yes, they all seemed very nice." She agreed, but refused to let him sidetrack her. "I just remember you used to put the TV on when you were lonely for home."

He shrugged. "Old habits die hard."

"And what about this big house? It's a total bachelor abode, but I have to think you were thinking of a family when you bought it."

"Sure." He shrugged. "I've always planned to have a family someday."

"Have you ever come close?" She bit her lip behind the words wondering where her head was at digging into his personal business. Except it wasn't her head asking, it was her heart.

"You mean besides you?" He sent another ball rolling. "No. Unlike you, I've never been close."

That's right, he knew of her marriage. To the dweeb. No surprise, really. Aidan was sure to have told him. And she may have protested the description before, but in truth it was incredibly accurate. Interesting that Rett's history lacked any serious relationships.

She still refused to believe she'd broken his heart.

"Back to Ryann's room." He brought them back on point. He swept the little girl up and headed for the stairs. "I suppose you want to convert the media room?"

"It's your choice, of course." She followed him. "But I suggest the office for Ryann's room. It's closest to your room for convenience plus it's at the back of the house so it'll be quieter. Then you have so much space downstairs, you could separate the pool table and the poker table with the media stuff and create three different entertainment areas."

Rett looked at her speculatively as he set Ryann down.

Skye rushed on. "You'll be surprised by how much paraphernalia comes with a baby. You may want to shift your desk into the workroom and make the empty room a library/playroom to contain it all and not let it spread all over the house."

Hands in his pockets he stared at her for a moment, rocked back on his heels and then forward. "Wow, that's a lot of work. We better get started."

He pulled out his cell phone and hit two buttons.

"What are you doing?"

"Calling in the muscle. Hey, Rick," he said into the phone. "Time to get off your lazy ass. I need some help." He outlined Skye's plan, promised some food and hung up. "Okay, grab your purse, we have some shopping to do."

Strapping Ryann into his Escalade, Skye's head spun at how fast everything was moving, especially when he took two calls from family before they cleared the block, one offering a crib, dresser and changing table, and a second telling him not to worry about the food.

"Sisters-in-law are the next best thing to TV remotes." He grinned at Skye and for a moment she saw the man she'd fallen in love with so long ago. She carefully looked away. Maybe this had been a mistake. Being drawn into the loving circle of the Sullivans was like stepping into emotional quicksand.

Rett's hand covered hers on the seat and squeezed, drawing her attention back to him.

"Tell me now so I can start preparing myself, are we painting the room some frou-frou color, pink or purple or such?"

"No." She laughed at his pained expression, happy for the distraction. "We can do the job with accessories. What color is the furniture?"

"Cherrywood."

"Nice. Head to Toys 'R' Us. We should find everything we need there."

CHAPTER SEVEN

TWENTY MINUTES LATER Rett stood in a baby aisle dedicated to little girls. Hands on hips he surveyed shelf upon shelf of princesses and fairies.

It was pastel color hell.

His home would never be the same. A little girl was going to change everything. Why couldn't Cassie have had a little boy? At least then he'd have some idea of what to expect. But a little girl was so out of his league.

He walked around the corner and immediately sighed in relief to be surrounded by blue, yellow, red and green. And it wasn't just that this was the boy's aisle. Give him primary colors every day. Jewel colors. They spoke to him.

"You're in the wrong aisle." Skye stood with her hands on the handle of an orange cart. Ryann sat in the seat.

"I know. I'm more comfortable over here."

"Well, you are a boy."

"Damn straight."

"But you're buying for a girl."

"Yeah, I get that." He scrubbed a hand over his neck. "I like the bolder colors."

"So pick a theme with bolder colors." She waved to shelves near her.

He surveyed the selections she'd indicated and shook his head. "These are brighter, but not particularly girly. What did she have in her room at home?"

"Cassie had her room done in full princesses. She even had a castle mural painted on the wall."

"Huh." Mulling the information over, he made his way back to the girl aisle. "Maybe we should go with that—it would be familiar to her."

"Oh. Do you think that's a good idea?"

A slight distaste in her tone drew Rett's gaze to her. "You obviously don't. Help me out here, Skye. I want to make the right decision. Or perhaps we should let Ryann choose."

"Ryann likes it all." Skye trailed her fingers over a row of plush fleece blankets. "Don't do the princesses. I think it would be too much of a reminder of other places, other people and might be upsetting. Choose something else."

"You're right." He hadn't thought of that. He frowned at all the soft and fluffy choices. "Why don't you choose?"

"Because it's your house. This is only the first of a thousand decisions. And this isn't even a tough one." She nudged him with her shoulder. "Plus you're the father of a girl, you better get used to it."

"You're taking way too much pleasure in this." He nudged her back. "You're supposed to be helping."

"So tell me the real problem here. What's really bothering you?"

"Maybe I'm taking on more than I can handle here," he confessed. "What do I know about raising a little girl?"

"A single man who grew up with five brothers?" Her gaze ran over him from head to toe and back. "Nothing?"

"Exactly. I'm crazy, right?" He rolled his head, stretching his neck, working at the stress building in his shoulders. "You warned me. I should have listened."

"Rett, stop." She held up a hand to halt his downward spiral. "You're the one who talked me into this."

"I know, but dolls and princesses, pinks and purples? I'm out of my realm here."

"So it's new ground. So what? She's female, a particular specialty of yours. You'll be fine."

"Very funny."

Skye sighed. "How unfair is this? You're the one who dragged me into this adventure and now you want me to rescue you from your folly. What did you say to me? Get over it already."

He flinched. "Ouch."

"Yeah."

"I'm sorry." And he meant it. This situation wasn't easy for either of them. They could at least have tolerance for each other. "That was the cold talking."

She inclined her head in acknowledgment.

"Look," she said, "all that's happening here is you're freaking out because your bachelor pad is morphing into a family home." She ran her hand over Ryann's soft curls. "You made the decision to raise your daughter. You convinced me it was the right thing to do. And you were right. Do you have all the answers right now? No. But don't let a few girly items stop you from following through on what you know in your heart needs to be done."

He chewed that over. "Maybe I am panicking a bit over all these pastels."

"Right. And I repeat that oh-so-famous advice: get over it. You're good with color, with design. Use your instincts."

"Right." He rubbed his hands together, refocused. "You're right. I can do this." At the end of the aisle he spotted some violet. And a bright green. "Now we're talking." He strode down the way, pulled out a blanket and held it up. A blonde pixie and her fairy friends smiled at him.

"Tinkle Bell."

He cocked a dark eyebrow at her. "Even I know Tinkle Bell. I like this. It's bright and cheerful. Exactly what I want for Ryann." He tossed the blanket in Skye's cart. "Show me more."

Three of Rett's brothers came to help out; an impressive number considering it was a weekday. Rick got there first, followed by Brock and then Cole. Brock's wife, Jesse, also came along.

The men put their muscles to use shifting furniture, Ryann was napping in Rett's room, and Skye helped Jesse with the food.

"I brought fried chicken along with all the sides." Jesse started pulling items from a plastic bag, releasing a savory burst of steam into the air. "With extra chicken and extra biscuits."

"Works for me." Skye watched Jesse move around the kitchen. The woman was obviously familiar with where everything went. "Does Rett have paper plates?" she asked opening a pantry door and peaking inside.

"Second cupboard from the left." Jesse gestured to the cupboard she meant with a nod of her red head.

"Here's the water, babe." Brock dropped a twenty-four pack on the island counter, kissed Jesse on the cheek and then headed down the hall to where grunts were coming from the media room.

"Water not beer?" Skye wondered aloud. She set the paper plates on the counter next to the new baby monitor and started putting waters in the freezer to get cold. The rest went into the refrigerator.

"Yeah," Jesse confirmed. "It's a weeknight, so once the work is done we'll all be on the road home. After we eat, of course."

"It's a well-stocked kitchen for a bachelor," Skye observed, remembering the cooking magazines she'd seen on Rett's coffee table.

"Rett likes to cook. And by that I mean he does more than grill meat on the barbecue." Jesse grinned at Skye.

"Which is about Brock's limit. Rett had the family here for Sunday dinner a couple of times this last summer."

"I thought Sunday dinner was always at Gram's."

"It used to be. But Rick changed that last year when Savannah was on bed rest while expecting Joey. He thought the company and camaraderie would be good for her and since she couldn't go to Alpine, he invited the family to his place. Since then we take turns, but we all go to Gram's at least once a month."

Skye knew it was those dinners that kept the family close. She'd always envied the Sullivans for being such a large family, but she'd felt she and Aidan were closer because there was just the two of them.

Now as she struggled to reconcile her brother's deceptions, she realized no matter how close you were to someone, they could still surprise you. And that she could only really depend on herself.

"I'm glad Rett has you to help him," Jesse said.

"You must have been surprised to hear he'd been a donor," Skye prompted.

"At first, yeah." Jesse closed the oven on the chicken. "But then I realized it was just like him. He's one of the best people I know. But he's still going to need a lot of help."

"I'm trying to help where I can."

"She needs both of you right now." Jesse assured her. "Just do me a favor, don't break his heart again. Brock tells me he was pretty torn up when you left."

She didn't wait for a response from Skye but headed down the hall toward the sound of the men at work.

Skye stared after her, slowly shaking her head. More talk of Rett's broken heart. She just didn't believe it. Brock hadn't even been around that summer. And Rett didn't let go of what he considered his and he hadn't put up any fight when she left.

It took her a long time to admit she'd wanted him to follow her, to fight for her. And when she finally realized he wasn't coming, she'd done something really stupid. She'd married Brad.

Shaking off the bad memories, she followed Jesse, ready to lend her muscle to the men's to get this project done.

Jesse stood just inside the door, hands on her hips, surveying the lack of progress in the media room. They actually had the games console on and were having a shoot-out.

Skye met Jesse's gaze and lifted both eyebrows.

Jesse placed two fingers in her mouth and let out a sharp whistle. Four heads whipped around, identical expressions of surprised guilt flashing across the similar features.

"Yes, dear?" Brock tucked his gun behind his back as if out of sight would be out of mind.

Jesse rolled her eyes at him. "Work first, play later. You can try it out in its new location when we're done."

Brock glanced at Rett. "Told you."

Rett shrugged. "I was up on you."

"And I had you both." Rick surged to his feet. "Let's get moving with this." He stepped to the end of the long section of the large sofa. "Rett, grab the other end of this. Cole, you want to pack up the entertainment center since you'll be reassembling it downstairs."

"Skye, we brought some boxes that might come in handy, can you grab them from our truck? It's parked in the driveway. Brock, let's look at what's involved with moving Rett's desk to the workroom." Jesse continued to organize the troops, and Skye welcomed the direction. She admired the other woman's easy manner with the men.

Everyone split up to handle the assigned tasks. Rett and Rick had trouble getting the big furniture down the inside staircase. But once they realized they could take it through the family room and down the stairs off the deck and then in through the sliding glass door, things moved quickly.

With the men focused, they had all the furniture repositioned in just over an hour. After that it was a matter of putting things in order.

While Brock assisted Cole in reassembling the entertainment unit in the new media area downstairs, and Jesse and Rick stuffed books into the bookshelves moved into the library/playroom, Rett and Skye dug out the food.

Ryann happily munched cereal pieces in the high chair someone had sent along.

"That went faster than I expected." Skye pulled the chicken and potato wedges from the oven.

Rett winked and flexed his biceps. "That's right, baby."

She laughed at him. "Please, you know you guys just

want to finish the game we interrupted." The microwave dinged announcing the biscuits were done. "Shall we take this downstairs?"

"The guys would love that." Rett cocked his head. "You wouldn't mind?"

"Of course not. It's comfortable down there. And you all earned it."

"Great. Let's do it then."

"Yeah, Jesse and I can watch—" Skye stole a potato wedge, biting off the end "—and then we can take on the winner."

Rett grinned. "I like the way you think."

For all Rett's indecision over the theme and colors, the room turned out spectacularly. The purple and green went well with the cherrywood furniture to create a foresty feel.

"Look at your new room, Ryann." Skye turned in a slow circle so the baby could see everything. "Do you like it?"

"Tinkle Bell."

"That's right." Skye kissed Ryann's soft cheek. "You like Tinkle Bell."

"Pretty."

Along with the bedding, he'd bought a lamp and a doll package with Tink and seven of her closest friends. Perched playfully throughout, the bright fairies brought life to the room along with a deep green rug and a fairy-tale throw over a rocking chair in the corner.

"This is my favorite part." Skye showed Ryann the

mural Rett had painted freehand on the wall next to the crib. The huge tree lush with branches and leaves fit the theme beautifully. And he'd dismantled the two mobiles she'd tried to tell him Ryann was too old for and hung the fairies and butterflies in the tree so they appeared to flit about.

It was hard to believe he'd done it all in a little over an hour.

Skye flicked one of the fairies, sending it swinging and the wings flittering. Ryann giggled. She held out her hand. "I want."

"What? You want to be a fairy?" Skye lifted Ryann over her head and walked her around the room. "You want to fly?"

Holding her arms out, Ryann screamed with glee. "I wanna fly."

"Whee." Skye made another revolution but stopped when she spied Rett leaning against the doorjamb. He looked a little bleak.

"Hey. Everyone gone?"

"Yeah."

"You going to be all right? It's a big change."

"I don't have a lot of choice, do I? No." He immediately held up a hand and shook his head. "Forget that. I'll get used to it. So what do you think? Not bad for a spur-of-the-moment effort."

"It's freaking fabulous." She bounced Ryann on her hip. "Love the tree."

"Turned out all right. Smell is still a bit strong. I'll

keep her in with me tonight. Come here, kiddo, you want to fly?"

Ryann practically leaped into his arms. He lifted her high and flew her around the room. Skye spread her arms out like the little girl and pretended to fly, too.

They dipped and bobbed, chased each other and flew side by side. Ryann's shrieks of joy and laughter were infectious and Skye found herself giggling as she frolicked and leaped around the room. Finally she collapsed into the rocking chair.

Ryann begged for more and Rett gave it to her. He was so good with her, so patient. What's more, he really enjoyed himself with her. Watching them together made Skye ache.

"Hey, I should go." She stood and wiped her hands down the sides of her pants. "I have an early consult tomorrow morning. Or do you want help getting Ryann ready for bed?"

"Thanks." He twisted Ryann around until she rode on his shoulders. "But we have a system. We're just going to grab a shower, brush our teeth and hit the sack."

"Very efficient." Okay, Skye was not going to think of Rett in the shower, she just wasn't.

"It's worked so far." He followed her into the living room where she scooped up her purse. "Listen, do you want to move in here?"

CHAPTER EIGHT

"WHAT?" SKYE DEMANDED. Clearly he couldn't have said what she thought.

"Uh…" He blinked at her almost as if he were as surprised by his words as she was. "That didn't come out right. I need a favor. It would just be for a few days." He clarified. "I have a conference to go to in New York. I'd wave it off, but I'm giving the keynote speech and getting an award."

"Well, I guess they might miss you then. When are we talking about?"

"Thursday."

"As in the day after tomorrow Thursday?"

"Yeah." He grinned sheepishly. "I know it's last minute, but it kind of skipped my mind with everything that's been going on."

"I'd like to help, but I'm booked the rest of this week. I have two engagement shootings and several appointments for family Christmas photos. Plus, I had two weddings last weekend, and there's putting together the digital presentations for all of it."

"I know it's asking a lot. And Jesse will take her

during the days when you have to work. Ryann will be fine because she'll have the kids to play with. But she's just getting used to being here. To me. I don't want to confuse her by putting her into another overnight situation so soon."

Skye bit her lip. "That makes sense."

"I know it's a lot to ask, but she knows you, loves you. You're the one constant she's had."

"Rett." She stood, and the throw slipped to the floor. Bending she picked it up, carefully folded it in thirds and draped it over the back of the rocker. "It's not that I don't want to help."

No, it was the thought of being back in his bed again that disturbed her, because even with the baby monitor the guest room really was too far away. There was something about the intimacy of sleeping in his bed that threatened her carefully crafted detachment.

"Hey, if you can't do it, I understand. I'll see if Rick would mind staying here." On his shoulders Ryann's head drooped forward until it rested against his. Mink dark hair blended into mink dark hair so it was impossible to tell which was father's and which was daughter's. Her blue eyes blinked sleepily.

"Oh, no fair." She referred to both his guilt free acceptance of her refusal—which of course made her feel guilty—and the emotional tug of seeing father and daughter bonding. He was trying so hard, she felt compelled to do more. After all, it wasn't like he'd be in the bed with her.

"What?" he asked, all innocence.

"Please," she mocked his virtuous stance. "Okay. If Jesse can watch her during the day, I'll do it. I don't have any weddings next weekend, so I can make up whatever I don't get done then. Thursday, right? When will you be back?"

"Late Sunday."

"Oh. Okay. Sunday is—"

"Ryann's birthday. I know. We'll celebrate next week after I get back." He raised his hand to Ryann's arm wrapped around his neck. "Is she asleep?"

"Yes, she's out."

"Ah." He tenderly pulled her around until he cradled her in his arms. "She may get her shower in the morning."

"Right. I'm going to go. I have things to do if I'm going to be back here Thursday. Do you want me to put a party together for Ryann?"

"Let me think about that." He shifted the baby to his shoulder and followed Skye. At the door, he caught her hand, stopping her before she stepped out. "Thank you for your help today. I couldn't have done it without you."

"Yes, you could. But Ryann would be sharing a room with a monster TV."

He grinned. "Probably. Ryann thanks you, too."

"See you Thursday."

After putting Ryann to bed, Rett showered and pulled on a pair of sweats. Deep in the closet he opened a safe behind a mock shoebox and pulled out a small jeweler's box. Flipping it open he stared down at a ring. He'd designed it over fifteen years ago up on Mount Laguna for the woman he loved. A two-carat round diamond sat in a tower of baguettes; he'd seen it as his love surrounded in a hug. Fanciful, but he'd been in love and he hadn't cared.

When Skye lost the baby and took off east, he hadn't believed it. He'd torn up the design and thrown it away. At the same time he'd been sure she'd come to her senses and come back.

Okay, he hadn't been prepared when she announced she was pregnant, knew he bumbled the proposal, but she had to know he loved her.

Surely within six months—a year at the most—she'd be in his arms again. That was why he taped the design back together and went to work, by the time she returned he'd have it ready.

But she didn't come back. Not for nine years. And Aidan made it more than clear she wasn't interested in picking up where they had left off. And of course he'd moved on. But he'd never forgotten that summer, never forgotten the love that burned so brightly between them. Or the child they lost.

He tucked the ring back in the safe.

But even as he set the digital lock, he realized he'd never stopped missing his best friend.

And she'd been a friend today, helping him past his bad moment in the girly aisle. She always saw him so clearly; better than he sometimes saw himself. The day had come together because of her; they'd accomplished so much. Okay, he was still adjusting and mourning his old life just a little. But he did like the media area downstairs. And most of all he liked what they'd created for Ryann.

Skye had been right; the baby needed her own space. And he'd needed to give it to her. The tree pleased him because Skye loved it. And Ryann, of course. Watching the two of them flying through the space he'd created made the whole day worth every chaotic moment.

He dove into the play and got carried away. Suddenly they were a family and he wanted it to last. He'd thrown out that comment about moving in, which was ridiculous.

Scrambling to find a plausible excuse, he remembered the conference, which provided the perfect cover. He had intended asking Rick and Savannah to take Ryann.

This would work out better. Just a friend helping a friend.

No doubt about it, Rett Sullivan definitely had her number, Skye thought as she meticulously framed her shot of the engaged couple against the fountain in the rose garden of Balboa Park.

The wedding ceremony would take place here in three months. It was a lovely spot, in a historical park full of lush gardens and museums. The Spanish Colonial Revival buildings made an excellent backdrop, especially at this time of day when backlit by the setting sun.

The truth was she loved having Ryann to herself.

The more time she spent with Ryann, the more time she wanted to spend with her. Secretly, Skye had feared knowing the baby was Rett's would affect her feelings for her niece; but, if anything, her feelings grew stronger each day.

Now that scared her. Because too often caring hurt. Over the years she'd taught herself not to care.

But from the very beginning Ryann had slipped past her guard.

Rett had blown her off when she mentioned a girlfriend or future wife, but the reality was it would happen at some point. Skye couldn't see herself being friends with the future Mrs. Rett Sullivan. Which meant Skye would have less access to Ryann.

She needed to begin distancing herself now, to prepare for the loss to come. Before Ryann needed her too much. And heaven help Skye, before she needed Ryann.

Rett kept suggesting Skye might marry again, but she doubted she ever would. Perhaps that's why she felt so strongly about being the last Miller, because she knew in her heart she couldn't trust enough to love again. Man or fate, one left and the other stole; either way she got her heart ripped out.

She framed the young couple again, this time the bride stood with her back to the groom's front with his arms wrapped around her. She looked up at her fiancé with a comment and a laugh. Skye caught that spontaneous moment of shared humor, of unfeigned love and knew it was a money shot.

She usually let the couples go through the poses they

wanted first. Once they got the more formal shots out of their systems it allowed them to follow their whims more freely.

Skye had had enough of the pain of loss to last her a lifetime. That's why she'd hardened her heart against Rett.

Thoughts of his muscles all soap slick and flexing as he washed that hot body in the shower may ignite her imagination, and her hormones, but that's as far as it went.

She called an end to the shoot, the couple relaxed and shared a final kiss, relieved to be done. Skye caught the simple caress. This was the only place for romance in her life these days.

Her head ruled her body and her heart. It may be a little lonely, but she was safe from hurt.

Dark had yet to yield to the dawn when Rett hauled his luggage out of the backseat of a cab and then paid the driver through the front window. "Thanks."

"Thank *you*." The cabby grinned when Rett waved off the change. And then he was gone before Rett could change his mind.

Rett was just glad to be home. He'd canceled his Sunday appointments, so as soon as he'd accepted his award last night, he'd changed his flight to a red-eye return. It put him home almost a day earlier than planned.

This trip gave him an opportunity to do a lot of thinking. And the more he thought the more he realized that this was Ryann's first birthday with him and he wanted to be home for it. Ryann might not know better, but he did.

And Skye did.

She'd mentioned putting together a party for Ryann again last night when he talked to her on the phone, but he didn't want a big production. He wanted to spend the day with his daughter. And with Skye.

He'd missed them both. It surprised him how much.

He left his luggage in the living room and headed down the hall. The door to Ryann's room was ajar and he stepped inside. She slept on her side, her dark hair curled against her pale cheek. She was the most awesome thing he'd ever seen.

She'd thrown off her covers so he tucked it back around her and ran his hand over the silky softness of her hair.

Sleepy blue eyes opened. Shoot.

"Hey, baby, it's okay. Go back to sleep."

"Daddy." He froze, his heart clutching at the whispered word, recognizing the significance of it.

He wasn't ready for this. But there was no going back now.

Shoving the rising panic down, he rubbed her back until her eyes closed and she sighed back into sleep.

Standing, hands braced on the crib rail, he stared down at his daughter. His daughter. He could do this.

The truth was he'd had her with him for just over a month, and he'd only been gone for three days, yet he missed the weight of her against him, her sweet smile, her simple company.

And Skye. She'd been a godsend. Just like in the girl aisle at Toys 'R' Us, he'd have been lost without her. Her family had been ripped away from her, and yeah he got that he was part of the problem there. But he'd done what he had to do. And even hurting she stepped up to help him. For Ryann, he understood that, but he benefited, too.

In spite of her protests he knew Skye loved Ryann. He was growing fond of her himself. They'd become a ragtag family. And he had ideas to make it more permanent. But that could wait.

Right now he just wanted his bed. And the woman in it.

Skye slept in his room. The rising dawn afforded him a clear view of her. Dark hair spilled across the dove-gray pillowcase, a shining contrast to her porcelain fine skin. She slept on her side with one bare arm and one bare leg hooked outside the comforter and his fingers itched to touch as longing heated his flesh.

He made a mistake coming in here. He'd only meant to check on her like he had Ryann, more as assurance to himself that she was safe and sound and where he expected her to be than anything else.

Now fatigue weakened his control. He didn't want to make his way downstairs to a cold and lonely bed. He kicked off his shoes as he started on the buttons of his shirt. He longed to sink into this bed—to snuggle up with this woman.

His woman.

He'd always thought of her as his; distance and

marriage hadn't made a difference, nor his own denials. In his heart she'd always be his.

When he tossed his jeans aside and moved to the bed in his briefs, he told himself he was in control. He only wanted to hold her as he fell asleep.

Sinking into the cozy comfort of the bed, curling up next to Skye's warmth, smelling the sweet scent of shampoo and woman tempted him to test the softness of her skin. Cupping her shoulder he ran his hand down the satin smooth length of her exposed arm thrilling to the exquisite feel of her under his touch. As he laced his fingers with hers, he pressed his lips to the tender flesh behind her ear and began a path of kisses to the corner of her mouth.

"Wake up, sweetheart," he urged her as he pulled her into him. "I'm home."

Oh, yeah, he'd lied to himself.

Skye woke in a sensual haze. She'd dreamed of Rett, that he'd come home early and crawled into her bed. It took only a moment to realize from the heat and muscle surrounding her that this was no dream.

"Rett?"

"I'm here, baby," he crooned against the side of her throat where his tongue danced over her skin.

"But—"

She didn't get to finish as his mouth closed over hers. Still half asleep she was no match for his sensual mastery. He stole her breath and her will with his gentle demand. Seducing, teasing he drew her deeper until she wanted to sink into him.

"Wait." She struggled to reach the surface, to make sense in a world gone suddenly crazy. "Why are you here?"

He pulled back, ran a finger down the side of her face. Passion and something more brewed in his eyes. "I missed my girls."

"But I'm not yours." The response was automatic, and necessary. She needed a moment to think, a moment to gather her guard. He gave her no time.

"You've always been mine." He corrected her. And proved it by claiming her mouth again, rougher this time, more urgent. He took her deeper, drove her up faster.

The taste of him, the feel of him were so familiar it took her to another time and place. A time of freedom and the freshness of love. It seduced her as much as the man. And then he did something with those talented fingers that had her arching off the bed, and she knew it was all about the man, his touch, his kiss, his total concentration on her.

He made her feel precious, cherished. Every stroke of his hand, every moist kiss, every rub of skin over skin dedicated to her pleasure. She gave as good as she got, glorying in the hardness of him, satin over steel, he was all male, all man and she reveled in him, clinging as he took her higher and higher until she soared with all the heat and brilliance of the rising sun.

* * *

The next time Skye woke she was snuggled in Rett's arms. She'd dreamed this scenario so many times over the years she pinched him to see if it was real.

"Ouch." He covered her hand over his chest trapping her fingers. "What was that for?"

"You deserved it. Sneaking into a woman's bed."

He tightened his arms around her. "It's my bed."

She shook her head, her hair catching in the bristle of his beard. "Not while I'm in it."

"Especially when you're in it."

She felt his lips against her hair and tried not to let the tender gesture affect her.

"Why are you home?" she repeated the question he'd dodged earlier.

"I told you, I missed my girls."

"Come on." She pleated the sheet over his abdomen, wanting to touch him, knowing she shouldn't. She needed to get up, to shower and start her day. The longer she let this go on the harder it would be to convince herself it had all been a dream. "What happened?"

"I'm serious. You were the one who reminded me this was Ryann's first birthday with me. I decided I wanted to be home for it."

"That's nice." And had everything to do with Ryann and nothing to do with her. But that was for the best. And fine, if he wanted to make this about Ryann, maybe Skye could get some answers. Holding the sheet to her breasts, she propped herself on an elbow, looked into his eyes and demanded, "What made you do it?"

He didn't pretend not to understand.

"Aidan was hurting."

She waited for more, and got nothing.

"That's all?"

He shrugged. "Yeah. Cassie wanted a baby and he couldn't give her one. He asked Rick and me if one of us would help. We drew straws, and I won."

"You won? Is that how you see it?" This was her brother they were talking about and it still felt like a betrayal.

"He was hurting," Rett repeated. "I'd do the same for any of my brothers."

"You can still say that after your panic attack in Toys 'R' Us?"

"Well, Aidan wasn't supposed to die. But yeah." He slowly nodded. "Toys 'R' Us was a momentary lapse. You talked me off the ledge."

"Rett—"

"Shh." Rett cupped her cheek. "I'm sorry this hurts you. Sorry Aidan didn't tell you. But it wasn't about you. I helped someone I loved."

That pretty much told her he hadn't even considered her feelings.

She rolled away, sat on the side of the bed. She had her answers.

"I haven't set anything up for Ryann's birthday because you said to wait, but we can probably put a pizza party or barbecue together for this evening."

"Skye." His hand covered hers.

She shook her head and pulled her hand free. "Pizza or BBQ?"

Silence, then, "Neither. Let's just keep it simple with the three of us."

Oh, that sounded nice. Too nice. Too intimate. "She'd probably love the rides at the pizza place."

"That place is so loud. How does a picnic at the bay sound?"

"Perfect." For Ryann. And it was her day. Skye wanted to argue but she'd just have to deal. "She had such fun with the wagon out at Gram's I got her one for her birthday. We can eat and then take her for a ride."

"Great. What should I get her? What do we still need?"

We? That wasn't the first time he'd used a plural pronoun.

"Pfft." The sound gusted out of her as he rose up behind her and kissed her on the shoulder. She tried to stand but his arm around her waist kept her in place. "She doesn't need a thing. Your sisters-in-law came over last night and threw an impromptu baby shower."

"Yeah?"

"I hope you don't mind." She glanced at him over her shoulder. "They figured I'd enjoy it more than you."

"They figured right. That was sweet of them."

"It was fun. They really are great. I like them a lot." Much as she tried not to.

"I'm glad. Skye, look at me."

"I really need to get up and shower." She tried to move his arm. "Ryann will be awake soon."

"This is important." With easy strength he pulled her back into the middle of the bed so she faced him. He stopped her fidgeting by lacing his fingers with hers. The seriousness in his voice made her brace herself.

"I stopped in Ryann's room on my way in. She called me Daddy." His voice grew husky and Skye knew it touched him.

"Shook you, didn't it?"

He barked a harsh laugh. "Hell, yeah."

"Better get used to it."

"I guess." He sighed. "Are you all right with it?"

She closed her eyes against the quick burst of sorrow; at the reminder Ryann would never know Aidan. But the truth was the little girl didn't even remember him. Plus Rett would be raising her; he deserved the title.

And it would make it easier for Ryann.

Did it hurt? Sure, it stung, but life went on. And she knew just how he felt.

"She called me Mama twice while you were gone."

"Ouch." He lifted her hand to his mouth and kissed her fingers.

"I know. I corrected her, but I didn't want to make a big deal of it." But it had been a red flag warning it was time to step away. This morning's little adventure just hammered that message home.

"Of course not," he agreed. "She doesn't know the significance. It's not that she's forgotten her mom. It's that you're doing all the things Cassie used to do for her. It's natural for her to place you in that role."

"And for you to be Daddy."

He lifted his gaze from their linked fingers to her face. "I wasn't going to do this now, but—"

"Tinkle Bell, Tinkle Bell little star." A little voice trilled through the baby monitor. "Up the sky."

Skye met Rett's gaze and they grinned at each other.

"Our girl's up."

"Sounds like." There was another plural pronoun. He talked as if they were a family, acted that way, too. It confused the heck out of her. "What were you saying?"

"I've been thinking—"

"Mama, Mama!" Ryann called and Skye knew the little girl would be standing in her bed, shaking the sides of the crib.

"Sorry." Skye sighed, both disappointed and relieved by the interruption. "There goes my alarm."

He laughed. "Funny woman. I'll get her." He kissed her, quick and hard and then rolled out of bed giving her a grand view of his prime backside. As he pulled on his jeans, he promised, "We'll pick this up later."

He went out and Skye flopped onto her back. What had she done? Making love with the man was not the way to keep him at a distance.

Wait. Correction, having sex. Love had nothing to do with what just happened in this bed.

"Hello, baby." Rett's voice came through the monitor, "Ret—Daddy's home. Did you miss me?"

Daddy. Things were changing so fast. And, yeah, he'd asked if it would bother her. She gave him points for that. It didn't mean it wouldn't take some getting used to. And he really took the whole Mama thing well. Too well?

Listening to them chatter, she wondered what he'd been going to say? Wondered if she wanted to hear more.

What had he been thinking? She, at least, had the justification of being half asleep when he joined her in bed. And it was still no excuse.

This whole situation was too complicated. These last few days with Ryann had been tough. Every moment she spent with the baby made it harder for her to resist the sweetness of her, the playfulness, the affection she gave so unconditionally. She'd lost those closest to her yet she retained her innocence, her joy for life.

Skye sympathized and empathized with the child. She wanted to protect her from the emptiness life had to offer. But that was Rett's job now. She'd done what she'd set out to do, help them to bond. They didn't need her anymore, which was good. Excellent. She'd have today and then take a step back. Soon she wouldn't miss them at all.

Right.

Being in his arms again took her to another time and place, to a time of love, and freedom, and hope for the future. She'd been so open then, so optimistic, ready to take on the world with Rett by her side.

Making love—having sex—gave her a vitality and sense of connection missing from her life. More than her body, he'd touched places she kept locked away from the world.

She perched on an emotional tightrope and one wrong move could send her toppling.

And why lie here rehashing it all when she should be taking this time to shower and dress? Was she hoping he'd come back and share her shower? The thought was enough to spur her to action.

She threw back the covers and ducked into the bathroom. Maybe she'd make it a cold shower. If she was imagining him under the shower spray with her, she obviously needed a little shock therapy.

CHAPTER NINE

RETT CHANGED AND dressed Ryann while Skye showered. And a fine job he did, too, putting her in purple jeans topped by a pink shirt with purple polka dots. Skye could throw in a sweater and a jacket and be ready for whatever weather they encountered.

"Ryann's grandparents will want to see her today." Skye told Rett when they were discussing their plans during breakfast. "They called me during the week to see if a party was planned."

"Sure, we can go by there before we go to the bay."

Skye bit her lip. "I really think I should skip that visit. It would hurt them to hear her call me—" she glanced at Ryann who sat in her high chair stuffing diced peaches in her mouth faster than she could chew, "—the M word."

Skye shook her finger at Ryann. The little girl just grinned and stuffed in another bite.

"Yeah, you're right." Genuine concern furrowed Rett's brow as he considered the matter. "Why don't I call them, see if I can go over there now. Then you could catch up on some work, or whatever, and we can leave for the bay when I get back."

"That would be great. I did want to get some proofing done today."

"I'll make the call."

The Gleasons were thrilled to have them come over so Rett headed out.

"Hey," she called and he stopped at the door. "I'll get Ryann's present ready while you're gone. Call to warn me when you're getting close to the house."

"Will do," he acknowledged. "Don't bother putting any food together. We'll stop at a deli and get everything we need." With a wave he stepped outside and closed the door behind him.

Glad to have time to herself, Skye packed her things and carried her bag to the car. She wanted to be able to make a quick escape at the end of the day. In fact, she saw no reason why she should need to go back in the house at all. That was good.

If she didn't go in the house, she couldn't end up in Rett's bed.

Next, she pulled the red plastic wagon out of Rett's closet and placed the large bow she'd bought right on the handle. Ryann would see it as soon as she came in the door.

At Rett's bidding Skye didn't bother with food, but she did grab some juice packets and a few snacks for Ryann. She could be picky and Skye believed in being prepared.

She'd set up a workstation at Rett's desk and she carried her coffee and cell into the office. Sinking into his comfortable leather chair, she opened her first file and within moments was lost in her work.

When her cell rang, she scowled at the interruption. How could that be when she'd barely begun? But a glance at her watch showed two hours had passed.

"Hello."

"We'll be there in three minutes," Rett informed her. "Or do you need me to drive around the block a couple of times?"

"No—" she hit Save "—I'm ready." That was just enough time to power down and pack the laptop in her car.

"Good. See you in a few."

Ryann's eyes popped wide as soon as she saw the wagon.

Thrilled with her reaction, Skye snapped a picture with her cell phone camera.

Ryann wiggled until Rett let her down and she scurried to the bright red wagon and clambered aboard. Grinning up at her dad, she demanded, "Ride!"

Skye laughed.

Rett lifted a dark brow in her direction. "I see how it is. You get the glory and I provide the labor."

She smiled sweetly. "You wanted to know what you could get her."

Quick and graceful as a cat, he was across the room and his mouth was on hers, hot and exciting.

"Daddy, ride!" Ryann demanded.

He lifted his head. "I've missed you." He gave her another quick peck and started to turn away.

Skye grabbed the front of his shirt, holding him where he stood. "What are you up to, Rett Sullivan?"

"Daddy!"

She narrowed her eyes at him. "She picked that up pretty quick."

"She's been practicing." She saw the quick flick of panic in his eyes quickly chased away by a smile. His fingers around hers pulled her hand free of his shirt. "I'll just pull her down the hall and back. Then we'll pack up and go. We can talk when we get to the bay."

"Oh, we will," she promised.

He responded with a predatory smile.

Secure in her new decisions she lifted her chin. He didn't make her nervous, or so she told herself, completely ignoring the goose bumps covering her skin.

Days like this were why Skye loved San Diego. Cloud speckled blue skies and a warm seventy degrees in early November, you couldn't find better anywhere in the world.

At the bay they found a patch of sunshine and spread a blanket.

"Ride." Ryann pointed to the Escalade where she knew her wagon waited.

"After lunch," Rett told her and pulled out a juice pack to distract her while Skye slathered her with sunblock. When she was done she pointed and said, "Look at the birdies."

"Birdies." Ryann's eyes got big and she shot off for a clutch of black birds feasting a short distance away. The birds took flight and Ryann gave chase.

"Rett."

"I'm on her." With a lithe surge of strength he rolled to his feet and strolled after Ryann.

While father and daughter explored nature, Skye put lunch together. From the deli they had a large sandwich and several tasty looking salads, plus fresh fruit and a few chocolate chip cookies for dessert. Their own feast.

When she had everything ready, she wrapped her arms around her knees and watched Rett with Ryann.

The little girl loved to run and she was leading Rett on a merry chase. Even at the house she'd run from her room to the living room around the coffee table and back down the hall. In the wide-open space of grass and sidewalk, sand and water she raced from one wonder to the next exploring this new world.

In a park active with people—and often their pets—walking, riding and skateboarding Rett followed, caught up, held back, and occasionally gave pursuit. Oh, how Ryann squealed then, her cries of joy sending more birds skyward.

Skye grinned even as her heart squeezed tight.

Finally Rett picked the baby up under one arm and carried her like a football back to the blanket.

"We're hungry," he announced as he held Ryann upside down.

"Hungy!" Ryann confirmed, one huge grin.

"Food demands a kiss." Skye tickled Ryann's belly

with two fingers and the girl screamed with glee, twisting in Rett's grasp.

Taking mercy on her, Skye leaned forward to give Ryann an upside down kiss and the baby wrapped her arms around Skye's head and gave her a huge, sloppy kiss. Laughing, she took the squirming girl from Rett and set her in front of her on the blanket.

Rett dropped down next to them.

"My turn." He wrapped a hand around Skye's neck and pulled her over for a heated kiss.

She pulled back, sending him a warning glare.

He winked and bit into an apple.

Ignoring him, she dished out the food and then pointedly focused her attention on Ryann.

"Hey." Rett held up his soda can. "I forgot to tell you I heard from Bourne, he said Child Services has completed their review of us and they've approved us as Ryann's guardians."

"That's great." Relief filled Skye as she bumped her water bottle to his can. Being under scrutiny had been unnerving. "So it's official."

"Yep. She's ours."

She nodded, emotion squeezing her heart and closing her throat. She really was free now.

Rett polished off most of the sandwich while Skye took small portions of the salads and shared with Ryann. The tasty fare seemed all the better for being eaten in the fresh air and sunshine.

After eating, Skye packed up the remains of their meal while Rett lay down with his arms under his head and dozed. Ryann sat next to him playing with his fingers.

"Daddy sleeping?"

Skye nodded. "You want to go play on the toys?"

Her blue eyes lit up, and she was off and running.

"Wait for me." Little bugger. Skye scrambled to her feet and trotted to catch up with the two-year-old. For the next thirty minutes she pushed, caught, herded and spotted the active child. Ryann had so much energy; Skye actually welcomed the sight of Rett waiting with the wagon.

"Come on, sweetie." She plucked Ryann from a slide and carried her kicking and squawking toward the sidewalk. She settled down when she saw Rett standing next to the bright red wagon.

"Ride!" She clapped her hands and wiggled to be released.

Thrilled with the child's joy in her gift, Skye set her on her feet.

Ryann ran to the wagon, clambered on board and demanded, "Go, Daddy!"

Skye met Rett's gaze in a moment of shared amusement.

Falling into step with him, they walked along in silence for a ways. Or more accurately, they wove and dodged their way through the foot traffic out on this beautiful day.

As they neared the information center, Skye heard her name called. It was a bride from a wedding she'd shot a month ago. She made introductions but when the bride asked for a few minutes to introduce Skye to her friend who was getting married in the New Year, Skye told Rett to go on and she'd catch up.

Skye loved to talk shop and she always enjoyed hearing a client was happy with her work. The bride and her mother both raved about the package Skye put together for the couple. The friend had also seen the work and was hooked before she met Skye. She mentioned her wedding date, and Skye told her to call next week. After a few more minutes, she made her excuses and headed after Rett and Ryann.

She must not have been as long as she thought because it didn't take her long to catch up. When she gained his side, and apologized for abandoning him, he waved it off and asked about her work.

"I love it. I do portraits and weddings. Every wedding is different because it's so much about the people involved. Every bride has her own fantasy about her dream wedding. And that's what I focus on, tuning into the fantasy and giving each bride her own experience."

"I bet you get a lot of referrals."

Enjoying his interest she nodded. "Yeah, most of my work comes from word of mouth. I give all my couples a gift certificate for their first Christmas photo. It's a way to remind them I do portrait work as well as weddings. A lot of people take advantage of it, and most end up buying more than the one pose."

"Pretty smart." He complimented her, but it was the admiration in his eyes that sent a tingle down her spine.

An older couple stopped in front of them, forcing them to stop, too.

The woman offered a sweet smile. "We saw you earlier when we walked by and I must say you have such a lovely family. It's just a joy to see."

"Oh, well…" Skye didn't know what to say. She didn't want to embarrass the woman by announcing her mistake. A glance in the wagon revealed Ryann had fallen asleep.

"Thank you," Rett said, graciously accepting the compliment as if it fit them perfectly. "You two make a lovely couple. I hope we're still holding hands thirty years from now."

"You flatter us." The woman laughed. "Keep that joy in your heart, and there's no end to what you can accomplish together."

"Thanks for the tip." Rett nodded an acknowledgment and began walking again.

Skye quickly caught up with him. "They were a nice couple. How could you mislead them that way?"

"Easy. They were a nice couple. Why embarrass them for jumping to an obvious conclusion."

"Because it's dishonest?"

"Not really. We are a family, just an unconventional one. Which I think we should change."

Skye came to an abrupt halt. "What are you talking about?"

He stopped and met her gaze over the length of the wagon, Ryann sleeping innocently between them.

"Exactly what I said. We're already a family. We should make it official."

"Official?" Skye's heart raced as a sinking feeling overcame her. No. He wouldn't do this to her again.

"We should get married."

And there it was. The most unromantic proposal ever issued. A strong sense of déjà vu sent her reeling back fifteen years to a time of crushing disappointment, of loss and pain and betrayal.

For a moment she couldn't breathe for the pain. When she could, she turned on her heel and walked away.

"Where are you going?" he demanded. "Don't you think we should discuss this? We're her guardians, it would be expedient, the perfect solution to this situation."

"I don't want to get married because of a situation." Certainly not because it was expedient. She didn't look back. And when she heard him behind her, she walked faster, and then began to run.

"Skye!"

No. Tears stinging her eyes, she picked up her speed putting time and distance between her and the pain nipping at her heels.

CHAPTER TEN

A SHORT CAB ride later Skye sat on a hillside with her chin propped on her knees. She loved this park, this place, where the world spread out before her. From this vantage point the sky stretched clear down to the bay. Or on days like today when the morning gloom had faded away and clouds floated off the coast, she could contemplate the vast Pacific Ocean as it reached for the horizon.

She often brought couples here for their engagement pictures. The grass and trees were so lush, the views so spectacular it was the perfect showcase for their love.

A light breeze dusted the bare skin of her arms and legs while the scents of grass, earth and roasting hot dogs floated on the air. Skye barely noticed the perfection of her surroundings as pain pulled her attention inward.

For as far back as she could remember she'd come here to celebrate life and to sulk away her woes. Today not even the peace and beauty of Kate O. Sessions Park soothed her soul. Today the fantastic views were blurred behind tears no amount of control could hold at bay.

Rett's duty inspired proposal shredded her emotions. And though she knew his actions stemmed from a deep sense of obligation and responsibility, Skye's understanding didn't reach to acceptance or forgiveness. Not for this.

She'd taught herself not to care, but this reached down to wounds tender from the past until she felt as if fate had slapped her in the face. And it made her angry she was so upset.

She didn't love Rett, didn't want a love match.

Yet the lack of emotion in his proposal cut her to the core. All those years ago she'd believed in their love—had convinced herself that the unplanned pregnancy would bring them together, that they'd be a family.

His dutiful proposal had been an icy bath of realization. Obviously what they had together wasn't special, not even close. And then it hadn't mattered any more and that had hurt even worse.

A large male body settled on the grass next to her, with a stroller parked next to him. In the hopes he'd go away, Skye ignored Rett. As much as it was possible to ignore a six-foot-plus man sprawled so close his heat ratcheted up the temperature of the mild day.

Lord, he smelled more delicious than the hot dogs.

After a few minutes he removed his running shoes and white socks. Then he tugged up his jeans, leaned back on the heels of his hands, and buried his toes in the green grass.

He didn't say a word, just sat quietly by her side. The

stillness from the stroller told Skye that Ryann must be sleeping.

Time ticked by but where, before, the sights and scents of the park hadn't distracted her, Rett now did.

She sneaked a peak at him from the corner of her eyes. He sat back absorbing the sun. The gold chain she knew held a St. Christopher's medal gleamed against the tanned skin of his throat.

He habitually dressed with style and flair. She thought of it as his artistic sense leaking to the surface. Which may be fanciful, but whatever. It was sexy. His confidence and the ease with which he moved were testaments to his self-assurance and self-mastery. He was all man and made no apologies for it.

Ten minutes passed, and then twenty. Why didn't he leave? Didn't he get the hint her answer was no?

She scooted over and turned to her left so she no longer held a view of his legs or his long, well-formed feet. Okay, it took all of twenty seconds to realize she'd made a mistake. Now she tortured herself with the question of whether he left or not.

Of course she knew he hadn't. Even though she'd opened the distance between them, she still felt him: a solid, immovable presence behind her. Plus he was too dogmatic, too perverse to make it so easy on her.

She forced herself to wait five minutes to give him a chance to get the message before turning to confront him. He wasn't there.

The pain of his desertion ripped through her, shattering the illusion of her control, of her indifference.

And now she cried, just placed her head on her upraised knees and let the tears flow. Sad tears. Angry tears, Confused tears. For the loss of Ryann, for the loss of her baby, for the loss of a friend.

Her body shuddered under the impact of emotion.

And then strong arms surrounded her, and she was pulled back against a hard, warm chest.

"I'm here, baby. I didn't go anywhere," Rett said against her temple. "I'm sorry. Ryann was stirring. I was just pushing her around to settle her down."

His forearm circled her chest; she wrapped her hands around him and hung on tight while she let the tears flow.

"I'm sorry," he repeated and she heard the sincerity in his voice. "I know I messed this up. It's because I already had it all worked out in my head. It makes perfect sense. We both care about Ryann. She knows and loves you. We're a family, Skye. Don't let my lack of eloquence stop you from considering my proposal."

"Oh, you're eloquent enough." The constriction around her heart confirmed that. She pulled away from his hold, swiped at her cheeks. "But marriage is just crazy talk."

"You're running scared because you don't want to get hurt again." He met her stare with a direct gaze. "I'm offering you a chance for a family without the risk of being hurt."

She froze, and then turned to face him with an accusatory glare. "There is no such thing."

"We've been doing it. You and I have created a family for Ryann. What we have together has been working. I'm just suggesting we make it legal."

"One problem with that," she snapped, on the defense. "Marrying you."

"Ouch." He cringed, and then lifted one dark brow. "You had no complaints this morning."

She put her finger in his face. "Do not throw that at me."

He wrapped his hand around her finger. "Can we at least talk about this like adults."

"As opposed to what?"

"I don't want to argue, Skye. I'm serious about this proposal. Talk to me." He dropped her hand and gestured to the sleeping baby. "I know you care about her. Isn't she worth a few minutes?"

Damn him for making this about Ryann. But of course she was the whole reason for the proposal. It was never about Skye, never about what was between them.

And that was a good thing, she reminded herself as she plucked at a blade of grass. Because there was nothing between them anymore.

Skye inhaled a deep, calming breath, letting it out slowly. She could make it through a brief conversation. And he was right; she couldn't just walk away. No matter how much she pretended to herself she could.

If she agreed to this—and she couldn't believe she was even contemplating it—it would be purely for Ryann's sake.

That was exactly what he was saying.

"I'm listening." She shredded the blade of grass into thin lengths. "You make it sound so easy."

"There's no reason it can't be." His hand settled over hers, stopping her nervous plucking with a gentle squeeze. "She's already lost her mother, having her aunt in her life is more important than ever."

Skye looked down at his hand on hers. Why was she fighting him so hard? A few minutes ago she'd been in total despair thinking she'd lost them both and here was Rett offering it all back to her.

"But I'm not—"

"You are. Legally you are her aunt, but also in your heart. Don't deny it."

She nodded her head, he was right.

"Ryann needs you, Skye. She needs a mother. While you were with your client, she announced she had to go potty. Knocked me for a loop-de-loop. But I realized I'm a single father, this was my job. After I pulled it together, I took her to the men's room. God, they're disgusting places."

He ran both hands through his hair, fisted them in frustration before dropping them to his lap. He sent her a pleading look. "Don't make me repeat that on a regular basis. It can't be good for her."

Skye stared at him both amused and appalled by his story. "I'm not going to marry you to keep Ryann from the men's room."

"It's a legitimate concern."

"Yes, but it's not a reason to get married."

"It's only one example of why she needs a mother."

Skye looked away. He'd hit on the one argument she couldn't defend against. She lost her mother when she was six and though she understood her father had done his best there were so many times when she'd longed for her mother. Someone to talk to, someone to listen, someone to help her move from girl to woman.

Skye could give that to Ryann.

He bumped her shoulder with his, drawing her attention back to him.

"We like each other."

"We hurt each other."

"The bathroom incident confirmed for me I was on the right track. She needs a mother." He repeated. He took her hand, played with her fingers. "I'd like it to be you. We've been friends forever. Yes, we have a history; but we're compatible and there's great chemistry between us. This could work."

She pulled her hand from his, tucked it into her lap. "I think you're simplifying our history. What about the fact I broke your heart?" Better to put it on him than expose her own vulnerabilities.

"We start with a clean slate. Leave love out of it."

She looked out over the bay, brushed her windblown hair out of her face. "We lost a child, Rett. I can't just wipe that away."

"No. That's not what I meant." A finger under her chin turned her head around, demanded she look at him. Regret darkened his gaze. "The loss of our child is a scar each of us will carry always, but it shouldn't keep us from moving forward with our lives."

"Maybe. I don't know." For Ryann's sake she'd put their differences aside these last few weeks, but she wasn't at all sure she could keep it up full-time.

"Mama." Ryann appeared in front of Skye rubbing her eyes. "I waked up."

"Yes, you did." Skye pulled Ryann into her arms. The little girl laid her head on Skye's shoulder and closed her eyes. Skye's throat contracted with tears she refused to shed at the display of total trust and unconditional love.

Rett ran his hand over the downy softness of Ryann's hair and then lifted his compelling gaze to Skye.

"Another child needs us now."

Weary in both body and spirit, Skye let herself into her apartment. She left her bag in the entry and carried her laptop with her to the couch. Plopping down, she kicked her feet up on the oversize ottoman and let her head fall to the back of the beige ultrasuede couch.

It felt good to be home. Or so she tried to tell herself. In truth it felt out of sync. She'd spent so much time at Rett's lately her own place seemed cold, impersonal. And too quiet.

She'd think about it.

That's what Skye told Rett in answer to his marriage proposal. Her head urged her to turn him down flat, but her heart wavered.

Who would ever believe when she used to hide from all the boys and men in her life to read a good romance she'd one day be living one? Ha. She was here to tell you there was nothing romantic about a loveless proposal.

But she wasn't looking for love.

She perked up at that thought. No, she wasn't looking for love.

She'd been considering this from the wrong perspective, as the young girl of the past, hurt by a dutiful proposal and looking for a happily ever after.

Skye wasn't that girl anymore. She was a strong, independent woman reliant on no one but herself. A woman with no plan to marry and start a family because she'd learned it was easier to be alone than to hurt.

And still Ryann had slipped past her guard. She'd been the only light in Skye's life since she lost Aidan. Much as she'd fought it, Ryann had won. Skye loved the girl with all her scar torn heart.

Taking care of Ryann, being close to her these last few weeks had brought joy to Skye's dull existence, given her purpose. She didn't want to lose that.

Rett's proposal changed everything.

She didn't kid herself. The two of them, father and daughter, were a package deal.

If she refused, the easiness of her and Rett's current relationship would end. Her access to Ryann would become limited at best. Skye could fight for her custody rights, but he was Ryann's father. The courts would side with him.

Rett had it in his head Ryann needed a mother. If Skye turned him down, she had no doubt he'd find someone else.

From the beginning her sense of self-preservation insisted on distance from Rett as the only safe way of dealing with him. She'd set that instinct aside to help Ryann. And look where it had left her.

She'd spent this morning in his arms.

And had it been so horrific? Yes and no.

Yes, because being with him exposed her vulnerabilities. No, because in his arms she felt alive as she hadn't in way too long.

Reaching for the remote, she turned on the TV, thoughtlessly flipping through the channels. Her mind was going in circles. She longed for a few minutes respite from the struggle in her head.

Emotional exhaustion took over and she fell asleep. An hour later she woke with a stiff neck, a growling stomach and a new resolve.

It was too late to protect her heart from Ryann. So the bottom line was Skye would do anything to keep Ryann in her life. She didn't love Rett, so a loveless marriage suited her fine.

But first she wanted to know she could put the past behind them. When she had the answer to that question, she'd agree to marry him. Or walk away.

CHAPTER ELEVEN

RETT SAT ACROSS from Skye at a traditional Mexican restaurant in Old Town. She'd called and asked him to meet her here alone. Obviously to discuss his proposal, but she wasn't talking, at least not to him.

Antsy, she munched on the chips and salsa and chatted with the water guy, the waiter, the mariachi band. Everyone but him.

The waiter swung by with their drink orders. Skye welcomed his appearance, gracing him with a smile and asking after the specials. She could talk as long as she wanted. Rett faceted beautiful gems from raw stones, he knew how to be patient.

He added his order for carne asada to her dinner selections and let the waiter leave before demanding her attention. "You're nervous, Skye. Am I so frightening?"

"Of course not."

"Then why are you avoiding me after asking to meet me here? I was hoping for an answer. You have a bad habit of leaving my proposals dangling."

She frowned. "What's that supposed to mean?"

"It means you left my last proposal hanging. And now you're stringing me along again."

Her scowl deepened and she looked like she wanted to argue but thought better of it. Good choice, how could she argue with fact?

"Right." She sipped her wine, swallowing hard as if taking medicine. "I'm not handling this very well."

"Handling what?" he asked, forcing her to get to the point.

She actually flinched. "Accepting your proposal."

How like Skye, when something mattered it was never simple.

"You're killing me here. It should be easy. All you have to do is say yes."

"That's the point." She bit her lip. "I'm not ready to just say yes. I have conditions."

He leaned back in his chair and crossed his arms. "Why am I not surprised?"

She frowned. "Are you angry?"

"No." Try frustrated. "I'm trying to understand what's going on here."

"We're having dinner and discussing your proposal."

He sat forward and caught her gaze with his. "I thought you were accepting my proposal."

"I'm inclined to accept your proposal. You know I love Ryann. But I need to know that you and I are going to work, too."

"I thought we proved how well we work on Saturday morning."

Her cheeks pinkened delightfully. "There's more to a relationship than sex."

"Arguably nothing more important."

"Oh, I could argue."

Yeah, he actually admired her ability to take any side of an issue and argue it intelligently. But this was one argument she'd lose.

"Are you saying you want a marriage in name only? Because that's not in the cards."

"No, that wouldn't be practical."

"On that we agree."

"But I would like a trial period."

"What kind of trial period?"

"One where we live together to see if we're going to be compatible."

"We know we're compatible."

"We were compatible. We've both changed."

"Not that much."

"I want this for both of us, Rett. We won't be doing each other any favors if a year or five from now we come apart at the seams." Earnest, her eyes pleaded with him to understand. "Yes, we have a strong foundation to ground us, but we also have a history that can trip us up. We've never lived together, and that's all I'm proposing. That we cohabit before we do anything official."

"How long are you talking about, because if you're saying yes, I'm ready to drive to the county office tomorrow."

"See I knew you were thinking of a drive-by wedding, but that's not in the cards, either."

"No? Since you're not real sold on it, I thought you'd want fast and simple."

"Wrong. I want pomp and ceremony. My first marriage was a civil ceremony, and I think the lack of a formal ritual was part of the problem. There was no sense of importance right from the beginning. And until I'm sold, this wedding isn't going to happen."

Rett sighed. Obviously she wasn't going to budge on her condition. Equally as obvious were the unsettled issues between them. He couldn't fault her for wanting to put all the ghosts of the past behind them.

"How long are we talking about?"

"I don't know." She bit her lip, not appearing entirely pleased by his capitulation. "A couple of months?"

"How about a couple of weeks."

"Weeks!" Her voice rocketed up an octave.

"Okay. Two and a half, but I want to announce our engagement at Thanksgiving. That should give you time to put a wedding together by the end of the year."

Once the decision was made for Skye to move in with Rett, he wasted no time in making it happen. Over her protests he hired movers.

At the end of two days, she did have to admit the team of four men and two women had made short work of the difficult job. Under her supervision they'd been fast, competent and respectful. Of course the fact most of her stuff went into storage helped. That part didn't bother her. Except for her photos and her mother's jewelry collection Skye had little emotional attachment to her things.

Before she was really ready for it, she was ensconced in Rett's guest room. A comfortable room, it still felt odd to think of it as hers. Once she put a few of her prints up, she felt more at home.

Rick and Savannah had them over for dinner the first night so Skye didn't have to worry about putting anything together for a meal.

Rett had promised she wouldn't be responsible for the cooking, but she'd believe that when it happened.

"I hear congratulations are in order." Savannah smiled at Skye over a simmering pot. She set the lid in place and came over to give Skye a big hug. "You are a lucky woman. Rett is a good man."

"Thanks." Skye bit her lip as she returned the hug. She should have known Rett would tell his twin. She wanted to say it wasn't official yet but held her tongue. "I'm not quite used to the thought yet."

"Did he rush you?" Savannah stepped back and gave Skye a sympathetic look. "Neither he nor Rick have any patience when they make up their mind they want something. And it's been clear from the beginning that he's had his eyes on you."

"He is persuasive." Skye picked up the knife next to a ripe tomato and began chopping it for the salad already started. "I'd have liked more time to make sure we've put our past behind us."

"Do you love him?" Savannah asked as she checked the bubbling chili.

Raw and vulnerable Skye looked at her with stark eyes. "I love Ryann. She snuck past my defenses, but beyond that, my heart is so full of fear I'm not sure I have more in me."

"Oh, Skye." Savannah stilled Skye's hand to stop her from cutting the tomato any smaller. "It's understandable for your guard to be up after losing so many people throughout your life, but like with Ryann, love doesn't always heed our fears. I can tell you I was not going to fall for a workaholic. Even when I got pregnant I fought my attraction to Rick, but it was a losing battle. He already had my heart, I just hadn't acknowledged it yet."

"I'd given up hope of having a family of my own—" Lord that sounded so pathetic.

"But you think this is your last chance." Savannah finished for her.

"Yes."

"I don't believe that's true, the heart has remarkable healing abilities if you let it. I've also found it can be sneaky."

Skye tilted her head. "Sneaky?"

"Oh, yeah." Savannah nodded emphatically. "Hope comes from the heart not the head. I think your rationalization is your heart looking for an opening to let Rett in."

"Oh my God." Skye's knees went weak and she sank onto a nearby stool.

"Here." Savannah thrust a glass of red wine into Skye's hands. "Drink this."

She heard the words but made no sense of them.

"Seriously." Savannah put her fingers under the glass and lifted. "You've lost all the color in your face."

Skye sipped, no taste registered but heat rolled down her throat. She choked. Coughed. Waved Savannah off when she pounded on her back.

"I'm fine," she assured the other woman. "Just a moment of sheer, terrifying panic."

"You've already agreed to try. My advice is to be open and give yourself a chance."

"*Me?* Not Rett?"

"Rett knows what he wants and he's made it clear. You're the one keeping yourself from moving forward. It doesn't have to be that way. You don't have to be afraid. Remember, you aren't alone anymore. You're a Sullivan now."

"Not yet." The protest was instinctive.

Savannah grinned and shook her head. "Rett has you in his home. He won't give you up now."

The next morning Skye wandered upstairs early with the thought of hitting Rett's home gym. The smell of fresh brewed coffee lured her into a detour by the kitchen.

How strange to open the cupboard and find her mug there. She'd been on her own for so long sharing a home would take some getting used to.

Ready-made coffee was a definite perk. She doctored

the cup with a splash of sweetened creamer and sighed over her first sip. Really good coffee.

Carrying the mug she made her way down the hall. All the doors were open, including Rett's bedroom. There was no sign of anyone, but a TV was on somewhere.

Skye peeked in Ryann's room. She slept peacefully, her dark lashes fanned across her cheeks. Skye quietly backed out of the room and turned to the one across the hall.

Light flooded the room through vertical blinds on the large picture window. A floor-to-ceiling mirror covered one wall reflecting the massive weight set in the middle of the room. And she'd found the TV, a forty-inch flat screen perched high above shelves heavy with barbells, sporting gear and towels. The room also sported a treadmill and a stationary bike.

After a few stretches, Skye climbed on the treadmill, set it for a moderate workout and started walking. When she looked up, she almost fell on her butt.

One of her photographs graced the wall in front of her. She'd taken the shot about a year and a half ago. Skye had been experimenting with shadows, and she'd caught headshots of her and Ryann when the baby was six months old. She leaned over the baby, kissing her softly on the forehead with the two of them silhouetted as dark shadows against a fuchsia sky. It had the evocative feel of a Madonna and child yet the brilliance of the sunset gave it a contemporary element.

Aidan had loved the shot as soon as he saw it, so

she'd blown it up, framed it and gave the picture to him for his birthday.

So how had it ended up on Rett's wall?

And did he know it was Skye in the picture? The shadowy profiles could easily be mistaken for mother and child.

"Good morning."

Flaming Cheerios! Startled by Rett's appearance Skye quickstepped to save her butt again.

"Good gracious, give a girl some warning next time."

"Sorry. You're up early." He walked to the weight set, sat down, reached for the tension bar and started working his biceps.

"Yeah but I'll be working here today." Mesmerized by the flex and flow of muscle, Skye's pace picked up as her blood heated. The man did look good. "I can keep Ryann with me."

"I've been through that with Julie at the day care center. We pay the same monthly fee whether Ryann goes or not, because Julie wants to encourage Ryann's attendance. She said it's best for her to stick to a routine."

"That's our modus operandi here at home so I guess it makes sense for day care as well." She turned the treadmill off and stepped down. Carefully keeping her eyes to herself she walked over and grabbed a towel.

"I'll drop her off on my way to work," Rett said, "but if you could pick her up this afternoon that would be great. I have some late meetings."

"I can do that." Skye draped the towel around her

neck. She nodded at the print. "Where did you get the picture?"

His gaze went to the photo on the wall and softened. "Aidan had it in his office in the downtown store. I asked Cassie if I could have it."

"It's a good shot of her and Ryann."

His arched brow and knowing gaze mocked her. "Do you think I don't know you when I see you, Skye?"

"It could be Cassie."

"But it's not." His glance went to the picture. "It's good work."

"Thank you. I was playing with shadows and I thought it turned out rather well."

Enough with the polite chitchat, she wanted an answer to the question burning in her since she first saw the picture.

"Why?"

"Why what?"

"Why this picture? Why in here?" Actually she understood him being drawn to the piece. It was a shot of his daughter he could enjoy without announcing his involvement to the whole world. But why place the reminder of that child in here, a room he used every day?

Especially when the picture included Skye. She didn't know what to make of it.

"I already told you, it's a good piece. I recognize art when I see it."

Though his response complimented her work it gave her no satisfaction. Not when she longed for insight into his emotions.

"Not the kind of art you usually see in a gym."

"It's a private piece and nobody uses this room but me." He flicked a glance over her sweat dampened sports bra. "Nobody used to."

Savannah's words about opening up and giving love a chance rang through Skye's head. How did she do that when Rett played his cards so close to the chest? She couldn't, so she picked up on his other comment.

"I didn't think you'd mind if I used the gym."

"I don't." No hesitation there. "This is your home now. You can do whatever you want. I'm just not used..."

"To sharing?" she supplied.

"The view." He grinned.

"Very funny." She rolled her eyes. "I'm going to grab a shower. What time does Ryann wake up?"

He glanced at the clock on the wall. "Anytime now. But go on. I'll get her."

"I'll be quick."

"Don't worry about it. She's easy in the morning."

Glad to hear it, Skye headed downstairs where she showered, dressed and threw on some makeup. She was anxious to join them on this first day together.

When she reached the kitchen, Rett and Ryann were already there and started on breakfast.

"Mama!" Ryann greeted her with glee. She sat in her high chair with a bowl of half-eaten scrambled eggs in front of her. "I eat."

"I see that." Skye kissed Ryann on the head. "Good morning, little pixie."

She tilted her head back her blue eyes big. "Wha, pixie?"

Skye pinched Ryann's tiny nose. "A pixie is a pretty little fairy."

Ryann laughed. "I a fairy."

"I'm a fairy," Skye corrected.

"Mama pixie, too?" Ryann clapped, eggs flying from the spoon in her hand.

Skye met Rett's amused gaze. "I guess I walked into that."

"Julie says our best strategy at this point is by example, and to stay away from baby talk."

Hand on her hip Skye faced him across the island. "Julie seems to have a lot of opinions."

He rounded the island until he stood over her. "Jealous?" He tugged on the end of her hair.

"Should I be?" she challenged.

"Never." He lowered his head and kissed her softly. "Good morning."

She licked her lips. "Something smells good."

Him. He smelled like soap, mint and man, an intoxicating mix, but she made a point of checking out the stove.

She heard a low chuckle then the press of his mouth behind her ear, making her shiver before he stepped away to grab a plate.

"There are eggs, bacon and biscuits." He handed her a glass of orange juice as he ran down the menu.

"Oh my. I usually keep it light, a slice of toast or a yogurt."

"Breakfast is the most important meal of the day."

"Smart as—rty" She checked herself with a glance at Ryann who had turned over her bowl and was hitting it with the spoon. "Since you went to so much trouble, I'll have a little of everything."

"Good catch." He nodded toward a large clear jar on the kitchen counter. "This is a no cuss zone. It'll cost you a dollar every time you slip up."

"Hmm. It looks like there's quite a bankroll in there."

Red colored his cheekbones. "Over a hundred dollars."

She laughed softly. "Are you getting better?"

"Yes, thank God, she's a little parrot." He handed her a plate and they sat down to eat. They talked about their schedules for the week, and Rett told her he was going to start adjusting his workweek to match hers.

His willingness to give up his traditional weekends told her how serious he was about making this relationship work. It gave her hope she'd made the right decision.

She insisted on doing the cleanup but first she took Ryann to the bathroom. Since she'd asked to go potty, they felt she was ready to continue her training. After they finished in the bathroom, Skye put on Ryann's socks and shoes and she was ready to go.

Skye saw them to the door. She kissed Ryann's cheek and handed Rett the backpack with Ryann's snacks. "Have a good day."

Rett wrapped a hand around her neck and pulled her

in for a kiss that made her wish he was coming home, not leaving for the day.

"Bye, dear." He bit her lip softly and then stepped outside and closed the door.

CHAPTER TWELVE

THE NEXT COUPLE of weeks flew by. And it turned out Skye's fears for her and Rett's compatibility were unfounded. Or unrealized, depending on which way she was swaying at the moment.

But their toughest test loomed ahead of them. In the backseat she had Ryann's diaper bag and a suitcase. The Gleasons had called and asked to take Ryann for a couple of days.

This would be the first time Skye and Rett were alone together overnight.

Sure they had alone time after Ryann went to bed. And yeah, Rett used every excuse he could devise to get his hands, lips, arms, or any other available body part on Skye, but he never pushed it beyond light petting because of his promise.

And because Ryann was usually around.

It would be interesting to see how things went while she was gone. The little girl acted as a magnate and a buffer. She drew Skye and Rett together and gave them something to focus on instead of each other.

Skye swung into the parking lot of Rise and Shine

Preschool and made her way inside. Julie, it turned out, was a little bit gray, a little bit plump and infinitely patient. She wore a bib apron, red tennis shoes and a perpetual, serene smile.

Ryann loved Julie. She loved her time at the preschool.

That was one decision Skye and Rett had gotten right. It encouraged her to think they may have a good partnership ahead of them. These last two weeks hadn't been completely terrible.

Rumors of Rett's cooking abilities turned out to be true. She'd seen the cookbooks and him working in the kitchen, but she'd had her doubts.

In the past he'd always been better at phoning in a take-out order than pulling out a pan. Plus she remembered he'd been waiting for a pizza delivery the first time she'd come to the house.

She liked to cook, too, even when it was only for herself. Having others to cook for added joy to her day. Meals became family time with Skye and Rett sharing the prep and cleanup.

Then it was playtime until Ryann's bedtime. Once she conked out, Skye and Rett were essentially alone. He'd told her he usually did chores or worked for an hour or two and then relaxed with some TV or a video game before bed.

Skye preferred to work during the week and save her chores for Mondays. Her first inclination leaned toward taking her laptop to her room and working there. But that plan defeated the bigger goal of testing their compatibility.

For the sake of harmony she'd set up a desk in Rett's workshop. And that's where their first dispute came up. She liked quiet when she worked and he always had white noise going, either music or the TV. Compromise came in the form of earphones. Except for the odd occasions when he serenaded her, something he didn't even realize he was doing.

No complaints from her there. Those spontaneous moments made her smile. And for all his obsession with TV, unless he had a sporting event he wanted to see he gave her complete freedom over what they watched.

"Mama!" Ryann ran to Skye as soon as she saw her and hugged her around the knees. "Tinkle Bell fly to the fower and hi."

"Really?" Only half understanding Skye ruffled Ryann's hair and said, "That sounds like fun."

"We watched the new Tinker Bell movie this afternoon." Julie explained as she strolled over. "Ryann is quite the fan."

"Yes, she likes her fairies," Skye confirmed.

"I pixie." Ryann swung Skye's hand and then ran off to chase a ball.

"She's happy here." Skye tracked Ryann's movements as she played.

"Yes, she's adjusting well. Her time here helps, but her sense of security begins at home. You and Mr. Sullivan should be proud of your efforts."

"We're trying." The woman's words of encouragement

eased something deep inside Skye. "Ryann won't be here for the next couple of days. She's spending some time with her grandparents."

"Thanks for letting me know." A scream filled the room. "Matthew, let her hair go. I have to go, see you next week."

"Yes." Skye watched Julie home in on Matthew and after freeing the blond locks clutched in his hand, advise him on the finer points of being a gentleman. From the look of Matthew, Skye wished her luck with that one. "Ryann, come on, baby, it's time to go."

Ryann came running and Skye carried her out to the car and strapped her in.

"I have a surprise. You're going to see Gammy and Poppa."

"Gammy?"

"Yes. You'll like that, huh?"

"Poppa."

"That's right. Poppa, too."

Clearly excited Ryann chattered away. Skye smiled, she was going to miss the little busybody.

Which brought her back to her earlier thoughts.

With the baby out of the house would she and Rett commingle or go to their separate corners?

Half of her said to retreat, but only half, which was surprising. The other half hummed with anticipation. And truly she didn't know if that was good or bad. So she decided to be open. To see what happened.

Turned out they got on fine. They worked together cooking dinner, talking about their day. Then Skye had work so she moved into the workroom while Rett put in some time in the gym. They ended the night with a duel of virtual bowling.

Rett won and claimed a kiss for his victory, a long, slow, tongue-twisting, knees-weakening kiss that made her sigh and long for more.

Instead she escaped into her room.

The hum that had stayed with her through the night grew in intensity to a full-blown tingle. She was in so much trouble.

The house was too quiet. After Rett left for work, the silence chased Skye from the house. She ran errands, picked up some groceries and finally the need to work forced her home.

She tried working at her desk in Rett's workroom, but the stillness of the big house stifled her creativity. She finally gave into the silence and turned on some of Rett's music. The classic rock, turned low, was exactly what she needed to fill the emptiness.

He'd never let her off the hook if he found out, but he wouldn't be home for several hours, and what he didn't know couldn't cost her later.

In the zone she put together two engagement presentations and sent off the links, shot off her website information to three referrals, confirmed the time and place for her weekend assignments, and printed out driving instructions for the venues she was unfamiliar with. If she got the chance, she'd drive out to the venue close to the time of the wedding to get a feel for the trip and the place.

"Look at you, jamming to the music."

Skye jumped at the sound of Rett's voice. She swirled around to find him leaning in the doorway of the workroom.

"Good gracious. Scare the bejeezus out of me, why don't you?"

"What's a bejeezus?" He lifted one dark eyebrow as his eyes laughed at her.

"I don't know, but that's not the point. Make a little noise next time."

He moved forward, tipped her chin up to give her a kiss. "And give you time to turn off the music? Why would I do that?"

"To keep from giving me a heart attack?" She pushed him away, aware of the hard feel of his chest under her fingertips.

She glanced at the wall clock, nearly six. Time had flown. Maybe a little music wasn't such a bad thing.

"I wouldn't want that. If I lose you, I'm back to raising Ryann alone again."

She froze. "That's not funny."

"You're right." He laid his forehead on hers. "I'm sorry. It's been a long day. And it's too quiet in here."

"That's why I had the music on."

"Let's go out tonight. Have a nice meal and relax. We could even go dancing, or to a club."

"Tempting. We kind of skipped the whole dating process." Which had suited her fine. She wasn't in this relationship for romance. But she did want it to work. Open, open, open, she silently chanted. And then suggested a movie.

Okay, it was a bit of a cop-out, but there was nothing wrong with taking baby steps.

"Huh." His sensual lips twisted. "Some chick flick?"

"Well, if you insist, but I was thinking of the new action movie."

He grinned and hugged her. "God, I love you."

Skye went completely still at the careless words. Because he couldn't really mean them.

She didn't want him to mean it.

When she thought of being open, she was looking for a companionable existence, a partnership with hot sex. Possibly leading to a brother or sister for Ryann.

Love didn't enter into it. She just couldn't handle the risk.

Hearing the silence stretch thin, she reached deep and pulled out a carefree laugh.

"You are so easy." She patted his chest and, without meeting his eyes, stepped back to her computer. "You make dinner reservations and I'll look up the movie."

Calm down, she admonished herself. He hadn't meant anything by the throwaway comment. The words just caught her off guard. Love wasn't something she sought but oh hearing him direct the words at her brought back memories. It felt good, familiar.

And it shook her to her core.

"I know just the place." He pulled out his phone.

"Find a time after nine. I'm going to shower and change and I want to be able to relax over dinner."

"Got it." But a full minute later she caught herself still staring at the search engine screen, thoughts of Rett wet and soap slick carrying her off on a mini fantasy hot enough to make her palms sweat. What was it with her and thoughts of Rett in the shower? She was obviously obsessed.

Clearing her throat, she wiped her hands on her pants and then typed in the information for the movie.

Great idea, the movie, the less she interacted with Rett tonight the better. Emotion threatened her control. Between missing Ryann and Rett's declaration she felt a little vulnerable and a whole lot rattled.

So of course he took her to Leone's.

The family owned Italian restaurant tucked into downtown La Mesa served traditional Italian favorites. Wine bottles hung from the ceiling and red and white checked tablecloths covered the tables.

It looked the same today as it had the last time she was here fifteen years ago.

"Do you come here often?" she asked Rett fighting off a deluge of memories.

Before and after they'd been lovers, this had been their go-to spot.

"Not without you."

She bit the inside of her lip. What did that mean? She'd come to realize she'd misjudged him. God, how young she'd been, how self-absorbed. She liked to think she would have rebounded and cut him some slack, recognized his confusion and instinctive proposal for what it was. He might not have said he loved her when he proposed but before that moment she'd believed he did.

"Gosh, how many hours do you think we spent in here?"

"Too many to count. Good times."

"Yeah." She remembered it all: the laughter, the long talks, holding hands across the table. She'd been so in love and the future had been something to think about later.

"Hello, my name is Irene. I'll be serving you tonight." A petite woman in a kelly-green T-shirt and a long gray braid stopped by their table. "What can I get you folks?"

He ordered for both of them, their standard fare from the past, a salad to share and two spaghettis covered with mozzarella, and a big basket of bread.

"Do you remember the time Ford tried out for the cheer squad in order to pick up the head cheerleader?"

She laughed. "And he broke his arm trying to do a flip? You guys razzed him for years."

"We still razz him." The stories went on from there. The food arrived and they both reached for a piece of bread. Over the next couple of hours they laughed and reminisced, ate and chatted. The time for the movie came and went.

And eventually the conversation came around to that

fateful summer. "Why Boston," he asked. "Why so far away?"

"I was hurt and running scared. Nowhere seemed far enough away."

"And did you find the peace you were looking for?"

"Not really. But I had school to concentrate on. And then I met Brad."

Rett rolled his eyes. "Your first marriage was a divorce waiting to happen."

"Why? Because he wasn't you?"

"Yes. You weren't meant to go back east, you weren't meant to meet him. You certainly weren't meant to marry him."

"At least he actually proposed to me and he wanted me for me. He didn't toss a suggestion at me because it was the practical thing to do."

"Well, forgive me for wanting to take care of you and our child. And I'm sorry my proposal wasn't romantic enough for you. You can attribute that to shock. It's not every day I'm told I'm going to be a father. It's a pretty big deal you know. At least for me."

"Of course it's a big deal." Somber, she rolled her wineglass in circles, angsting over the past. "I was shocked, too. And scared. But I knew you'd be there for me."

"Did you?" It was almost an accusation. "You seemed to be disappointed in what I offered."

"I didn't want a proposal based on duty. I thought there was more between us."

"You didn't give what was between us a chance. You

ran away and then married the first man to show an interest in you."

He was right. She hadn't given them a chance. She recognized that now. And if they were going to have a future together, she had to forgive Rett in order to move on.

"Look, if you expect me to admit marrying Brad was my biggest regret, I can't do that."

"I guess that says it all." Rett scraped back his chair and stood up. He pulled out a couple of twenties and threw them down on the table. Next he tossed down the keys.

"Rett, wait." She tried to stop him, to explain. "I'm trying to tell you—"

"I've heard enough. Take the Escalade. I'll find my own way home." He turned and walked away.

And Skye let him. Damn his stubbornness. If he couldn't wait for just a moment, couldn't let her finish, he didn't deserve to hear what she had to say.

CHAPTER THIRTEEN

IT WAS AFTER one when Rick dropped Rett off at his house. He climbed out of the car and leaned down to say, "Thanks for the ride, and lending an ear."

"No problem," Rick said easily. "You'd do the same for me."

"Anytime."

"Love you, bro. Word of advice, don't talk to Skye until tomorrow when you're cool, calm and sober."

Rett glanced at the dark house. "I'm safe. Lights are out, looks like she's in bed. Night." He closed the door and rapped on the top of the car in a sign Rick was good to go.

Rick drove off and Rett started for the house.

He'd blown it tonight. Running off like a spoiled brat. But the thought of Skye with another man made rage run like molten lava through his veins. Always had, always would. And tonight hearing her deny her marriage was a mistake just set him off.

He loved her. Honestly, he didn't think he'd ever stopped.

When he said the words today, they just came out,

natural and heartfelt. He'd felt her go still against him. Was that because the words meant something to her or because they didn't?

He remembered what she'd said about her ex. *"At least he actually proposed to me and he wanted me for me. He didn't toss a suggestion at me because it was the practical thing to do."*

That cut deep. Because, God, she was right. He'd blown his proposal. And he'd made the mistake not once, but twice.

He, whose brothers all claimed there wasn't a woman he couldn't charm, lost all finesse when it came to asking the big question of the one woman who'd ever mattered.

He needed to make it up to her. Big time.

And in the back of his head Rett planned his next move.

He wanted to give her something romantic and sentimental. Something she'd remember forever.

He needed the ring.

Letting himself in the house, he frowned when he realized Skye had left the front door unlocked. He may be simmering over her refusal to acknowledge her mistake in marrying pretty boy Brad, but he'd never risk her safety.

A light clicked on across the room. Dressed in a pink tank and polka dot pajama bottoms Skye sat curled up in a chair. His gut clutched. Fresh faced and hair mussed she never looked more beautiful.

So much for Rick's advice to put off talking to her.

Looked like he had little choice. Still he'd try to waylay her. He was sober enough, but he didn't want to make another mistake.

"Probably not a good idea to talk now. I've had a couple of drinks."

Skye lifted one bare shoulder and let it drop. A deceptive move because she had no intention of letting him slip away again without saying her piece.

"We'll talk in the morning." He nodded but didn't move.

She stood and started toward him. "Marrying Brad *was* a mistake," she said softly as she walked ever closer. "It was wrong, but not my biggest regret. Not by a long shot."

His shoulders went back and his nostrils flared. She knew he was on the brink of leaving, but she held his gaze imploring him to stay, to listen.

"Walking away from you was my biggest mistake, what I regret most in life. Even more than losing our child. I loved you so much, it destroyed me when I lost you."

Satisfaction and something more flared in his eyes. "You didn't have to go."

"It felt like I did." She reached for his hand, laced her fingers with his. "I'm sorry. I was young, and I needed someone to blame. You were convenient."

When she lost the baby, it fast froze all the heightened emotions she'd been experiencing, the sharp disappointment and sense of failure, the loss of life and hope, the betrayal of duty over love. She'd run, burying all those harsh feelings, never bringing them to the surface allowing them to heal.

"I was young, too," he allowed. "And, okay, a little high-handed. I guess you have a right to feel like I was trying to railroad you. But I just wanted to take care of my family."

"I'm beginning to realize that. And that I didn't make allowances for your shock." Her gaze lowered to their linked hands; his so much larger and stronger than hers but capable of great gentleness. "I had time to think and to adjust—but unfortunately I built up impossible expectations."

"Not impossible." Threading his fingers through her hair, he tilted her face up to his forcing her to meet his gaze. "I just needed time to catch up. Fifteen years later I'm finally there."

"I'm trying to say I can't offer you love."

"Skye—"

"No." She shook her head. "Something broke in me all those years ago. I don't have it in me anymore. Maybe if it hadn't happened so close to losing Dad, it might be different. I don't know."

"But it's been working. Us with Ryann. You love her. Now isn't the time to run scared."

"I don't know," she repeated, stepping away from him. "I wanted this to work. Ryann is important to me. You…are important to me. But I don't know."

"I do." Rett cupped Skye's elbows and drew her back to him. She was so used to protecting herself she didn't even realize how far she'd come from the stiff woman who sat in the attorney's office two months ago. She was thawing and he wouldn't lose her now.

"We've been a family these last couple of weeks. We've clicked. Ryann has settled into a regular routine. I've settled into my role as father. And you're the settling influence responsible for it all. Ryann and I need you."

"I don't want anyone to get hurt."

"No one is going to get hurt." He'd make sure of it. "Because nothing has changed. We're still friends joining together to raise a child in need of a family. We can do that."

"But you said—"

"What?"

"Earlier today." Suddenly uncertain she licked her lips. "You said you loved me."

He frowned as if thinking her words over; he'd known that had shaken her. Shrugging dismissively he said, "What if I did? I care about you, Skye, or I wouldn't have asked you to be my wife."

"But—"

"No buts. You want to be a part of Ryann's life. We've proved we can get along. Let's do this."

Terror gripped Skye, because God help her, he had her. She did want to be a part of Ryann's life. And she did care about Rett. As long as she continued to protect her heart, she truly believed they could have a good life together.

He didn't even seem to remember saying he loved her, didn't seem to give it any weight, just accepted the affection between them as a solid foundation for a marriage. And that eased her mind. Low-key she could handle.

"A couple of drinks have made you quite eloquent."

He grinned. "So my sweet-talking is working?"

"A little, yeah."

"Good." His eyes lit with blue fire making her heart race. He lowered his head and then stopped and she found herself rising onto her toes, meeting him half-way. She opened her mouth under the slant of his, welcomed the sweep of his tongue over hers.

Moaning, she wrapped her arms around his neck enjoying the hard length of his body against hers. Letting her guard down, she offered no protest when he hooked an arm around her waist, lifted her off her feet and walked down the hall to his room. All while he continued to kiss her.

She smiled against his mouth when he set her on her feet. "This is cheating."

"Not if you say yes." He unzipped the back of her gray dress.

"Yes," she said, lowering to her feet and staring into his passion darkened eyes.

"Oh, baby." He kissed her temple, the corner of her eye, the curve of her cheek and worked his way down. "I've wanted this every minute of every day since we last made love. Actually, from before that."

"I've wanted it, too," she confessed, closing her eyes and arching her neck giving him access to continue his march of caresses. "But I mean yes, I'll marry you."

He lifted his head and a primal satisfaction lit his gaze. In minutes he had them both stripped and on the bed.

"You won't be sorry," he whispered in her ear. And then he promised, "I'll do everything I can to make you happy."

"Just make love to me. That's as happy as I can stand to be."

He lifted himself above her. "Skye—"

She didn't let him finish. She twined her arms around his neck and pulled him down to her.

"Now," she demanded, not wanting to think beyond the moment. She bit his lip then soothed the bite with a sensual flick of her tongue.

With a groan he took control of the kiss, of the embrace, of the loving. He cherished her slowly, thoroughly, using his hands, his lips, his body to take her beyond happy to ecstatic.

"Skye and I would like to announce we're getting married." Rett made his announcement at the end of the Thanksgiving blessing after everyone had said what he or she was thankful for this year.

Chaos erupted as exclamations, congratulations and hugs were exchanged. Questions of when and where came from several directions and Rett held his hand up and someone banged a spoon against a glass to get everyone's attention.

"Skye wants a formal church ceremony and I want it soon. So we've decided on a Christmas wedding."

The men groaned and the women sighed.

"A Christmas wedding, how lovely." Gram rounded the table and drew Skye into a hug. "My dear, welcome," she softly stated. "I'm so glad you two found your way back to each other."

Skye didn't know about that; but she hung on tight, appreciating the official welcome to the family. It meant a lot to her.

"There's not much time, we need to get planning," Savannah said, rubbing her hands together.

"December is our busiest time of year," Rick reminded Rett. "Skye, you know I love you. But can't this wait until the beginning of the new year?"

"Hey, I didn't complain when you took off on your honeymoon after the London opening and left me to handle all the resulting publicity." Rett sent his brother a dark look. "I'm not waiting. I don't want to give her a chance to change her mind."

"Now it comes out." Brock laughed. "You're afraid she'll come to her senses. Maybe we should all head down to the church right now."

"Don't give him any ideas," Skye protested. "I had to fight hard to talk him out of dragging me down to the courthouse."

"No, this is a great idea. This is different." Rett wrapped an arm around her waist and pulled her close as he jumped onto the suggestion. "The family is all here. We can run down to the church and have Father Paul perform the ceremony right now."

She turned to face him, patted him on the cheek.

"Not going to happen. For one thing there's the little matter of the license."

Chagrin wrinkled his brow as that sank in. He lowered his head, giving her a hard kiss. "First thing Monday morning we're taking care of that little detail."

"Sit, everyone. Eat." Gram called the family to the table. "We can continue to talk over dinner. We have much to be thankful for this year."

"Are you sure you don't want to move the date up?" Rett whispered in Skye's ear as he led her to her seat next to his. "It would make Rick happy."

"It's my wedding. But if you'd prefer to make Rick happy…" She trailed off and turned a cold shoulder.

"Vicious." He grinned and leaned down to her ear again. "You just try to shake me loose."

"I'm not going anywhere. And neither is the wedding. Unless you want to give me more time?"

"Oh, no." He ran his thumb over her lips. "We agreed on Christmas."

"I thought so." She settled in at the table and to the family she explained their reasoning. "We know Christmas is a busy time for everyone, but we figured we'd already be together and already be going to church—so the wedding would just add to the day."

"And it will," Savannah assured Skye as she maneuvered around Rick so she sat next to Skye. "Now, I know you already have some thoughts on what you want to do. Spill. Have you decided on your colors?"

"I have to go with Christmas colors. I'll have to see

what I find, but I'm thinking of a creamy ivory for my dress and a rich burgundy for my attendants."

"Wait, I can't hear." Jesse picked up her plate. "Trade places with me," she demanded of her husband.

"Me, too." Sami stood and motioned for Alex to move.

This started a full shift of the seating arrangements as the women shooed the men to one end of the table while they gathered around Skye to listen and plan.

Under the table Rett squeezed her hand before he gave up his seat to Gram.

Skye squeezed back. It was hard to believe she was the focus of so much attention.

For a few minutes she sat frozen as her ideas were picked up, approved and new options for other elements were suggested and bandied about. The easy friendship and obvious affection were a little hard to accept for someone who'd spent so many years dodging intimacy of any kind.

Savannah looked at Skye with concern and she realized she'd been quiet too long. With a sigh she forced herself to relax. These were her sisters now. Her aloofness had not kept them at bay, and it felt petty to deny their participation when she was dying to talk wedding.

But before she jumped into the fray she had a request to make. She laid her hand over Gram's on the table.

Gram returned the gesture and added a smile as she patted Skye's hand.

"Gram, will you walk me down the aisle?"

Tears flooded Gram's loving blue eyes. "Oh my dear. I'd be honored."

Rett sat on the couch in the media area, a classic Christmas comedy turned down low on the big screen. Skye slept curled in his arms.

He'd turned the movie off, but the lack of sound had caused her to stir and she needed the rest. She'd been burning the proverbial candle at both ends, and sometimes in the middle, these last few weeks.

Who knew December was such a big wedding month?

He ran his fingers through her silky black hair, loving the softness of it against his skin, loving the weight of her snug against him. Loving how she always made time for him and Ryann even while shooting two or three events a week, planning their wedding and preparing for Christmas.

He'd lived here for five years and never had a Christmas tree. This year he—they—had two: one in the big picture window upstairs and one down here. He glanced to the corner where lights twinkled merrily and Santa bobbed, swayed and smiled from every angle. Toys, snowflakes, colorful bulbs and silver bows made it a cheerful, festive tree.

No longer a bachelor pad, this was a home where a family lived.

The effort was taking a toll on Skye, and he didn't like seeing her so tired. She'd been dismissive of a honeymoon. Probably because she considered their marriage a thing of convenience and didn't feel it rated a honeymoon.

She was wrong on both counts.

Their marriage couldn't be more real for him. And he longed to steal her away for some quality alone time, just the two of them focused only on each other.

The action on the screen caught his attention and he laughed at the antics of the actors.

Sure they'd miss Ryann, but adult time was important, too.

Yeah, look at him now. How he'd clung to his bachelor ways. In spite of his backward thinking, he'd fallen in love with Ryann. Lord, Rick had been right about how huge it was. There was no beginning or end to his love for her.

Or for Skye. He hadn't been prepared for that. Even when he acknowledged his love to himself, he hadn't known how big his feelings would grow.

He ran his thumb over the naked ring finger of Skye's left hand.

She was an incredibly giving lover, passionate and responsive, except for the tiny piece of herself she held back. After they made love, he felt the distance grow between them even as she lay in his arms.

He knew she feared losing another loved one and she'd convinced herself that if she didn't love, she wouldn't get hurt. And that may well be true, but that wasn't truly living, either.

And, he realized, it wasn't good enough for him. For

a while he'd thought it would be enough to just have her in his life, but he didn't want part of her. He wanted all of her.

He loved her too much to settle for less than her whole heart.

His two attempts at a romantic proposal had fallen victim to their hectic schedules. He'd taken to carrying her ring around with him in the hopes of finding the perfect moment to propose.

It was two days until Christmas and their wedding was scheduled for after the Christmas Vigil service. Time was running out. Tomorrow night they'd be staying at Gram's, and Skye would be tucked in a room far away from him. He had to find his moment, because this was too important to mess up.

He needed to know she loved him before the Christmas Eve mass, because if the answer was no, there'd be no wedding.

"Everything is going to be so beautiful tomorrow," Savannah said around a yawn. "I can't believe you pulled this wedding off in less than a month."

"I had a lot of help." Skye climbed the garland-draped stairs beside her friend. And her Matron of Honor. Of course Rett had asked Rick to be his best man. The twins spent a lot of time together so Skye and Savannah had grown close. It was only natural for Skye to ask Savannah to attend to her at the wedding. And she'd been invaluable in pulling the rushed event together.

Savannah shook her head. "You did most of the work. This was genius, by the way. A lovely ceremony shared with the community, followed by your wedding night, and then a family Christmas with the added benefit of a wedding cake. It's nothing short of brilliant."

"It's everything I've ever dreamed of in a wedding."

"You had a vision, which made decisions easy. Thank goodness. Your schedule's been brutal. How does it feel to know tomorrow you'll be the bride?"

Good question.

"Surreal." And that was an understatement. Her emotions were all over the place. She was excited and apprehensive, eager yet dragging her feet. Happy one moment, anxious the next.

Skye still couldn't believe she'd let Rett talk her into this marriage.

He'd said he'd make her happy and he did. Too happy. Their old friendship had clicked back into place. They talked about anything and everything, laughed at the same things, had fun together and with Ryann.

He went wild with the Christmas shopping. Skye took delight in watching him obsess. Come Christmas morning Ryann would be one happy little girl. The men were downstairs right now, putting together bikes and dollhouses.

It was all too perfect.

Skye wanted this so much, which made her fear it all the more. Already she cared too much.

Savannah stopped at the top of the stairs. Tears

welled in her eyes, and she reached for Skye's hand and held her tight.

"Gram is so moved you asked her to walk you down the aisle. That was so generous of you. Thank you."

"Savannah, she's honoring me." Skye squeezed Savannah's hand. "I have no family. Gram is the closest thing to a grandmother I've had since I was six. There's no one else I'd consider asking."

"Oh. You're going to make me cry." She caught a tear on her finger and wiped it away.

"Don't do that. You'll start me going, too. And I refuse to have red, puffy eyes for my wedding."

"Hey, I'll be right there beside you."

"Right. Quick, what do we still have to do tomorrow?"

"Actually we're as ready as we can be. The flowers will be delivered to the church at two o'clock. And the cake arrives at three. Then we're all set until it's time to dress for the ceremony. The hardest thing we have going for us at this point is keeping the cake out of reach of the children—and men—until Christmas day."

"I hope it all goes so easy. In my experience there's always some glitch or another to liven things up. Makes for some memorable shots."

"This is how I look at it, as long as it's not major, it just adds to the adventure."

"Hmm." Skye chewed her lip. "I'm not sure wedding and adventure go together."

"Sure they do." Savannah gave Skye a hug. "Don't you know? Marriage is the adventure of a lifetime."

"Oh. My stomach just dropped to my feet."

Savannah laughed. "You and Rett will be fine. Friendship is your foundation—it's a good basis for a marriage."

"I hope it's enough. How do you know for sure?"

"You don't. You trust each other and work together. The rest falls into place." Another yawn stole over Savannah. "Well, I'm off for bed. Get some beauty sleep, tomorrow is going to be a long day."

"I'm so tired, there's no way I won't sleep tonight. Good night."

"Night." Savannah turned away, and then stopped. "Skye, you're wrong, you know. We're your family now."

CHAPTER FOURTEEN

FAMILY. THE Sullivans were very big on the whole notion of it. Skye supposed it came from losing their parents when they were so young. It caused them to bond in nature as well as blood. And Gram was the glue that held them all together.

Skye sat on the bed in the guest room at Gram's, smoothing lotion into her skin and admiring the poinsettia and candles Gram had arranged on the dresser top. She'd added a touch of Christmas to every room in the house. To Skye it was a visual show of the woman's love for those in her life.

The house was already full. Skye and Rett both had rooms and Rick, Savannah and little Joey had another. Gram had taken Ryann in with her. The two of them got on like peanut butter and jelly.

Tomorrow more people would join them. Rett's brothers from the city, Brock and Ford, and their families planned to arrive in the afternoon, and then stay over after the wedding. And Alex and Cole would pack up their families and come over at the crack of dawn so everyone could open their gifts together.

Christmas morning was going to be huge.

How did Gram do it? Skye wondered. How did she open her heart so much when the risk of loss was equally as great? Skye couldn't even think of the affection she had for Rett and Ryann without freaking out.

Something hit the window, causing Skye to jump. Silly. Probably a tree limb moving with the wind. She set the lotion on the nightstand and rubbed her hands together and then over her elbows. Another sound came, this one a distinct knock on glass.

What?

At the window, she pushed back the curtains. She shook her head at the sight of Rett perched on a ladder outside. He helped her push the window open.

"Fool, what are you doing," she demanded, "trying to make me a widow before I'm a bride?"

"I have to talk to you and this is the only way I could get you alone."

"Well, it'll have to wait. You're not supposed to see me before the ceremony on the day of the wedding. It's bad luck."

"It's a quarter to midnight. I have fifteen minutes. Plus, I believe we make our own luck. That's part of why I'm here."

"Well, at least come in. It's freezing out there. And I don't want you to fall."

"I can't." He smiled, a self-deprecating grin. "The ladder is the romantic part."

Romantic? She grinned. "Are you going to ask me to elope? I'm afraid it's too late for that."

"You know I'd marry you anywhere, anytime. You wanted a formal family wedding, so tomorrow I'll be waiting."

And there, Skye realized, was the real romance. Yes, sneaking into her room the night before the wedding was a romantic gesture. But the real romance was in giving her the wedding of her dreams.

"It would be even more romantic if you came inside where I could kiss you."

"You convinced me." He climbed up another step. The ladder shifted against the wall.

Alarmed, Skye reached out and grabbed the steel sides.

"Careful."

Finally he slipped a leg and then his body through the opening. Once inside, he wrapped her in his arms and claimed his kiss.

"That's better." He sighed against her mouth. "I'm sorry I didn't give you the romancing you deserved. I didn't think of it because what I have with you is real. I don't have to manufacture a good time."

"Oh." Her heart melted.

"And you may have saved me from the ladder, but it's too late to save me from a fall. I've already fallen. For you."

"Crazy man. What are you talking about?"

His eyes turned serious and he took her left hand, carried it to his mouth and placed a kiss on the back of her fingers. "I love you, Skye Miller. Would you do me the honor of being my wife?"

Stunned speechless, Skye stared at his beautiful face, at the love shining strong in his bold blue eyes. Here was the proposal she'd always dreamed of, and it made no sense at all.

"Rett, I've already agreed to marry you."

"You agreed to what you think is a parenting partnership. I know that's the suggestion I tossed at you. But it's not enough for me, for us. I love you and I know that scares you, but I'm asking you to take a chance on me. On us."

"Rett, you know I care about you."

"Skye, you love me just like you love Ryann. You're just afraid to admit it. You're afraid it's inviting more loss into your life. But you can't live life afraid, or you're not living at all."

"Don't do this, Rett."

"We deserve to find happiness, Skye. I know I messed up fifteen years ago. I should have followed you, but I was arrogant and hurt and I thought you'd come back. I'm not making the same mistake again by not saying the words, of not claiming you." He opened her hand, and she felt the heat of his breath, the press of his lips to her palm. "I love you."

He fumbled for something in his pocket and when he opened his hand in it sat a red velvet case. He flipped it open to display a diamond engagement ring, a magnificent round diamond in a tower of baguettes.

"Please marry me."

"Oh my God."

She immediately recognized the ring from the

description Gram had given her. He'd designed this ring the summer she'd lost the baby. Gram said he never made the ring, but he had. And he'd kept it until now, because it was her ring.

Her heart contracted, expanded, terrifying her.

Even as she gazed with longing at the ring, she shrank back, putting her hands behind her.

"It's beautiful." She lifted her gaze to Rett's, blinked him into focus. "I don't know if I can give you what you need."

"I do," he said with confidence. "You're the strongest woman I know. Look at what you've accomplished in your life. You've been hurt and you've dealt with it by shutting down your emotions, but even then you stepped up when Ryann needed you."

"I don't think I could survive losing you again," she whispered.

"Life doesn't come with any guarantees and I can't promise I won't die. But I can promise we'll have a good life together in the time we have."

He set the ring on the window ledge and cupping her face in his hands, he drew her close to slant his mouth over hers. His tongue traced the line of her lips, seeking entrance. And when she gave in, he kissed her tenderly, so sweetly it was a demonstration of love, of respect and devotion.

"I want you for my wife. What I don't want is for the mother of my children to be afraid of life. And I don't believe that's what you want for Ryann."

She shook her head. She'd never thought of her insecurities in that way before. Of course she didn't want Ryann to live life afraid to try, afraid to love.

"Yes, it hurts when we lose someone important to us. But I wouldn't give up a minute with anyone I lost to save myself the pain."

She bent her head, thinking of the times she'd foolishly wished for that very thing; but it wasn't true, had never really been true.

"I said we make our own luck—we do that by grabbing every moment of happiness we can every day." He lifted her chin on the back of his fingers until her gaze met his. "I've never stopped loving you. And I believe we were meant to be together. If what we have ends tonight, it will hurt. What's the difference between hurting now and hurting later?"

"Rett—"

"No." He laid a finger over her lips. "Don't answer. Show me. I love you. I hope you love me enough to fight for us."

He kissed her hard once, twice, and then left through the door. Skye bit her lip, her wistful glance going to the beautiful ring sitting on the window ledge, a ring he'd made just for her.

Christmas Eve dawned crisp and clear with no forecast of rain or snow. Gram's became bride central while the men all gathered at Cole's. Because their only chore was to get themselves dressed and to the church on time, the men were on wrap and toy construction duty. Which meant the women had the kids with them.

That worked for Skye; otherwise she'd have no break from their fussing. On one hand she loved every moment of the fuss and bustle of being a bride, but on the other hand she still struggled with the question of whether she'd be walking down the aisle or not.

After Rett left last night, she'd plunged into a dark hole of despair.

She was the fool.

She was kidding herself thinking she could control her emotions. In this, it seemed he knew her better than she knew herself. It wasn't simple friendship and affection she felt for Rett.

She loved him, with her whole heart and soul.

But like a frightened child she didn't see what she didn't want to see. Acknowledging her feelings would mean she had to act on them. Fight or flee.

Her first instinct was flee. Feeling raw and exposed, all she'd wanted to do was run, to protect the shallow, isolated world she'd created for herself.

She'd pulled out her suitcase and threw in all her belongings ready to run away just like she'd run fifteen years ago. It was the empty space that stopped her. Space taken up with Ryann's things on the trip out.

Staring into the half full bag, Skye realized that's how her life would be if she gave into her phobia, empty and only half an existence.

She hadn't taken flight, but she hadn't unpacked either.

Now she stood alone in her room gazing at her reflection in the full-length mirror. Behind her the house was quiet, the Christmas tunes turned off, everyone but Gram and Skye picked up and taken to the church.

She'd been given this moment to gather herself and prepare for the ceremony. A moment she very much needed. She'd been on autopilot most of the day as her mind waged war over what her heart wanted and what her head feared.

Unless she risked everything, she lost everything.

Oh, she had no doubt he'd let her see Ryann, to have her custodial rights. But it would be like divorced parents trading off every other weekend. Awkward time spent being polite to each other at special occasions.

But that would be safe wouldn't it? And that's what she wanted, wasn't it?

Tired of the constant brain battle she took a deep breath and determined to turn it off. She actually focused on the mirror and saw her reflection.

And oh, God, she was beautiful.

The sleeveless, square-necked dress was a rich ivory fitted through the beaded, dropped bodice that flared into a full skirt with a deep burgundy sash tied into a bow low at the back. The sheer train flowed to the floor from the back of the sleeves. A shallow cascade of miniature ivory roses entwined in pearls and lace pulled her hair up and back on the left.

She truly felt like a princess.

Suddenly she wanted nothing more than to see Rett's face as she walked toward him down the aisle.

And that, she realized, was her answer. Life was better with Rett in it.

A knock sounded at the door and then Gram stepped inside elegant in a tea length, dusky rose suit and deep burgundy hat that exactly matched Savannah's dress and Skye's sash. She stopped and clasped her hands together.

"Oh, my dear, you are radiant."

"Thank you." Skye beamed; she knew she did because the smile came from the center of her soul.

"Rett is a very lucky man." Gram's gaze went to the suitcase set in the corner. "He is lucky, right?"

Skye inclined her head. Obviously he'd warned his grandmother Skye may bolt. And she'd said nothing all day. Or had they all been talking and speculating behind her back?

Her uncertainty must have shown because Gram stepped forward and took her hands.

"No, my dear Skye. Rett spoke only to me and I have respected your privacy." Her smile held a sly edge. "We are a close family, but we all know how to keep a secret. You'll find it can be quite aggravating at times."

Skye hugged the older woman. "I'm the lucky one to be marrying my best friend, a man who understands my insecurities and loves me anyway." Tears welled up and she tried not to blink and wreck her makeup as she confessed to the woman who would understand better than anyone else. "I love him very much."

"I know, dear." Gram handed her a tissue from the box on the dresser. "I never had any doubt. Now don't cry or your eyes will clash with your sash."

Skye laughed and dabbed at her eyes. "We can't have that."

"Shall we go? Alex is waiting to take us to the church."

Her heart jumped with excitement and anticipation. "I'm ready."

Townspeople filled the small church to capacity. The well wishes of the congregation truly touched Skye. During the mass she, Gram, Alex and his family had sat at the back of the church while the rest of the family sat up front with Rett.

Tiny in size with no more than twenty pews, the church made up in presence what it lacked in space. Cole had provided lush pine wreaths, poinsettias and creamy roses from his nursery, bringing the scents and colors of Christmas alive throughout the whole church.

Majestic columns, three on each side, marched toward the altar, creating shallow alcoves filled with tables holding candles and statues. Candlelight enhanced the dim lighting, bouncing off the stained-glass windows, reflecting back jewel colors, which reminded Skye of Rett.

How apropos for their wedding to take place surrounded by sparkling jewels.

From where she stood in the shadows of the vestibule she saw Rett standing tall and proud, and oh so handsome, at the front of the church beside Father Paul.

Her love for Rett swelled so big it pushed out all doubts. He'd called her strong and tonight she believed.

And she'd cherish every minute with him, no matter how many or how few, with no regrets in the future.

Because he was worth it.

When the service had ended, nobody gave up his or her seat except the Sullivans involved in the wedding and those seats were quickly filled. Music swelled as the organist began the wedding march.

"This is it." Savannah handed Skye her bouquet of dark red roses. "You really called a winner here. The church is spectacular, the people are having a ball, you look beautiful and that man loves you. Merry Christmas."

After a quick hug, Savannah turned and began the procession into the church.

Beside Skye Gram offered her arm. "Ready?"

"Suddenly impatient." Skye grinned, taking Gram's hand instead. "I want to run up there and claim my man."

"Oh. Dear, I much prefer we walk."

"Let's get going then."

The minute she cleared the door and met Rett's gaze across the room, Skye saw nothing else, only him. His blue eyes blazed with desire and an undeniable, overwhelming love. She went warm all over as everything in her responded to his call of devotion.

And suddenly she was there and he was taking her hand, drawing her next to him in front of the priest.

"You made it," he said, his eyes caressing her.

"I never stopped loving you, either," she said simply.

Something hot flared in his gaze.

The music stopped and Father Paul stepped forward. "We are gathered here tonight—"

"Sorry, Father," Rett interrupted him. "There's something I have to do first."

Before she could wonder what Rett was up to, he closed the distance between them, dipped her over his arm and kissed her, telling her without words how glad he was to see her.

The congregation erupted in applause and a few ooh's and ah's. Savannah giggled, Rick hissed, the Father mumbled.

Slowly Rett brought them upright again. Skye smiled against his mouth. "Now that's romantic."

"I'm just getting started." Rett took a half step back, and never taking his eyes from her face nodded for the Father to proceed.

Father Paul cleared his throat. "Dearly beloved, we are gathered here tonight to join Skye Miller and Rett Sullivan in holy matrimony."

* * * * *

CLASSIC

Quintessential, modern love stories
that are romance at its finest.

COMING NEXT MONTH
AVAILABLE DECEMBER 6, 2011

#4279 KISSES ON HER CHRISTMAS LIST
Susan Meier

#4280 RUNAWAY BRIDE
Changing Grooms
Barbara Hannay

#4281 FAMILY CHRISTMAS IN RIVERBEND
Shirley Jump

#4282 FLIRTING WITH ITALIAN
Liz Fielding

#4283 NIKKI AND THE LONE WOLF
Banksia Bay
Marion Lennox

#4284 THE SECRETARY'S SECRET
Michelle Douglas

*Lucy Flemming and Ross Mitchell shared a magical,
sexy Christmas weekend together six years ago.
This Christmas, history may repeat itself when they find
themselves stranded in a major snowstorm…
and alone at last.*

*Read on for a sneak peek from
IT HAPPENED ONE CHRISTMAS
by Leslie Kelly.*

Available December 2011, only from Harlequin® Blaze.™

EYEING THE GRAY, THICK SKY through the expansive wall of windows, Lucy began to pack up her photography gear. The Christmas party was winding down, only a dozen or so people remaining on this floor, which had been transformed from cubicles and meeting rooms to a holiday funland. She smiled at those nearest to her, then, seeing the glances at her silly elf hat, she reached up to tug it off her head.

Before she could do it, however, she heard a voice. A deep, male voice—smooth and sexy, and so not Santa's.

"I appreciate you filling in on such short notice. I've heard you do a terrific job."

Lucy didn't turn around, letting her brain process what she was hearing. Her whole body had stiffened, the hairs on the back of her neck standing up, her skin tightening into tiny goose bumps. Because that voice sounded so familiar. *Impossibly* familiar.

It can't be.

"It sounds like the kids had a great time."

Unable to stop herself, Lucy began to turn around, wondering if her ears—and all her other senses—were deceiving her. After all, six years was a long time, the mind could play tricks. What were the odds that she'd bump into *him,* here? And today of all days. December 23.

Six years exactly. Was that really possible?

One look—and the accompanying frantic thudding of her heart—and she knew her ears and brain were working just fine. Because it was *him.*

"Oh, my God," he whispered, shocked, frozen, staring as thoroughly as she was. "Lucy?"

She nodded slowly, not taking her eyes off him, wondering why the years had made him even more attractive than ever. It didn't seem fair. Not when she'd spent the past six years thinking he must have started losing that thick, golden-brown hair, or added a spare tire to that trim, muscular form.

No.

The man was gorgeous. Truly, without-a-doubt, mouthwateringly handsome, every bit as hot as he'd been the first time she'd laid eyes on him. She'd been twenty-two, he one year older.

They'd shared an amazing holiday season.

And had never seen one another again.

Until now.

Find out what happens in
IT HAPPENED ONE CHRISTMAS
by Leslie Kelly.
Available December 2011, only from Harlequin® Blaze™

SUSAN MEIER

Experience the thrill of falling in love
this holiday season with

Kisses on Her Christmas List

When Shannon Raleigh saw Rory Wallace staring at her across her family's department store, she knew he would be trouble…for her heart. Guarded, but unable to fight her attraction, Shannon is drawn to Rory and his inquisitive daughter. Now with only seven days to convince this straitlaced businessman that what they feel for each other is real, Shannon hopes for a Christmas miracle.

Will the magic of Christmas be enough
to melt his heart?

Available December 6, 2011.

Harlequin®

American ★ Romance®

LAURA MARIE ALTOM

brings you
another touching tale from

When family tragedy forces Wyatt Buckhorn to pair up
with his longtime secret crush, Natalie Poole, and care
for the Buckhorn clan's seven children, Wyatt worries
he's in over his head. Fearing his shameful secret will
be exposed, Wyatt tries to fight his growing attraction
to Natalie. As Natalie begins to open up to Wyatt,
he starts yearning for a family of his own—a family
with Natalie. But can Wyatt trust his heart enough
to reveal his secret?

A Baby in His Stocking

Available December
wherever books are sold!

Snowflake Bride

JILLIAN HART

Grateful when she is hired as a maid, Ruby Ballard vows to use her wages to save her family's farm. But the boss's son, Lorenzo, is entranced by this quiet beauty. He knows Ruby is the only woman he could marry, yet she refuses his courtship. As the holidays approach, he is determined to win her affections and make her his snowflake bride.

Available November 2011
wherever books are sold.

www.LoveInspiredBooks.com

LIH82891R